My Name is Mrs. John Singer

LISA G. SAMIA

Destiny Whispers Publishing, LLC
San Clemente, California
www.DestinyNovels.com

Author Copyright © 2020 by Destiny Whispers Publishing, LLC
LISA G. SAMIA, Author
MY NAME IS MRS JOHN SINGER / Destiny Whispers Publishing, LLC
Copyright © DESTINY WHISPERS PUBLISHING, LLC

First Edition -- March 4, 2020

ISBN-13 # 978-1-943504-34-3

Executive Editor, Formatting & Cover Art Design by:
Leslie D. Stuart, Creative Director, Destiny Whispers Publishing, LLC

Destiny Whispers Publishing, LLC
San Clemente, CA
www.DestinyNovels.com

My Name is Mrs. John Singer

It was early July, 1865.

The sequel to "My Name is John Singer" continues the fictional story of John Wilkes Booth who is hiding in plain sight and married to nurse Emma Dixon. While residing in Richmond, men who doubt his identity come to reveal John Singer as a fraud.

A bullet meant for John strikes Emma, shot from the gun of Doctor Henry Bradley. He is desperately in love with her and doubts John Singer's identity. Believing he killed the woman he adored, Henry fires the gun at his own temple.

With danger lurking, now they must escape Richmond for there are still men who wish to reveal the truth and bring John to justice.

"My Name is Mrs. John Singer" opens under the guise of night with John and Emma hiding at his childhood home of Tudor Hall in Bel Air, Maryland.

Asia has gathered the family in secret. It is time Mary Ann Booth knew her son is alive. John feels repentant for his crime, regrets his old ways, begs their forgiveness and assistance.

Will the family help, or turn their backs on John?

A review from author & playwright, Eric Swanson, co-author of the New York Times bestseller, *The Joy of Living*. Also book and lyrics for the play, *EDWIN: The Story of Edwin Booth*:

"*My Name is Mrs. John Singer* is work of wonderful imagination and freshness. Lisa G. Samia has crafted a moving novel that, by turns suspenseful and surprising, is illumined by love."

Acknowledgements:

To my husband, Jim, whose support and love
made all of this possible

Misty Michele Crites Long, thank you for your continued
friendship and love of all things John Singer

The Goldstein Family, a beautiful and special family
with love and gratitude, thank you

Jeff Ross and Reel Video Group, thank you for
your support and excellent work

Seharut Suankeow of SS & Co. Media,
my Publicist & Media Strategist

Leslie D. Stuart, Creative Director & Executive Editor
of Destiny Whispers Publishing, LLC

Terry Alford, Historian and Author, friend and supporter

Eric Swanson, Librettist for EDWIN,
The Story of Edwin Booth and co-author of the
New York Times bestseller, the Joy of Living

Jane Kosminsky, Artistic/Executive Director of Great Circle
Productions, Inc., & Faculty, The Julliard School

Cheryl Sard and Kathleen Taylor,
my dear, loving and supportive friends

To my mother

Helen L. Gentile

and

To my mother-in-law

Mary M. Samia

CHAPTER ONE

Tudor Hall in Bel Air, Maryland

"Johnny my child, is it really you?"
~~ Mary Ann Holmes Booth

It was early July, 1865.

The mid-summer rain fell lightly upon the tin covered roof of the Gothic revival home situated on the expansive acreage near the Maryland hamlet town of Bel Air. The faint tapping sound coming from the second floor broke the solemn silence of the family gathered downstairs in the shadows of the living room. This night the great hearth, normally offering warmth and light to the center of gatherings, bore no flame. Instead the latticed windows of Tudor Hall were open to the night, the summer rain bringing a slight breeze that was sweet, fragrant and heady.

The great family room where the hearth laid silent found members of the Booth family gathered under the guise of night bearing the dark burden of secrets too unspeakable for the garish light of day. The only light illuminating their stern faces came from the two oil lamps placed over the long mantle. The pale illumination flickered with the wet humid breeze as it drifted through the air, casting sad shadows across the portraits of the handsome family proudly displayed upon the hearth mantle.

The candlelight almost seemed to shudder across the Booth family matriarch's face, perhaps in fear or shame. Once a joyful sight, tonight the portraits appeared forever frozen in time, memories of happier days and happier times.

A melancholy sigh permeated the quiet as the broken-hearted mother studied the pictures of her adult children.

So much had changed.

Too much.

She paused at the mantle, seeing the one photo that brought a harsh sting to her eyes. Fingers trembling, she picked up the small portrait of her most favored child.

"Johnny," she whispered in sorrow as her thumb caressed the image of his handsome face. Aching inside in ways no mother ever should, Mary Ann Booth held the picture clasped to her heart. Her shoulders stooped with shame and her countenance twisted in pain as the reality of his heinous deed once again tore through her heart.

Her memory of three months ago, that terrible night in mid-April at Ford's Theater, in Washington D.C. was still so raw and painful. The decision her son made had shocked and changed everything for not only the Booth family, but for the whole United States.

Tonight under dark of night, her loved ones were gathered together in secret, coming home to Tudor Hall. The country house normally held a special place in all their hearts, but now the dark residence was a sad reminder of all the family had lost.

Knowing they were waiting, Mary Ann swallowed her own sorrow and bravely raised her head to look at her beloved children Junius, Edwin, Rosalie, and Asia. Yet, she still clutched the picture of her son, Johnny.

"I am here with you now at your insistence, coming back to a home that for me has been forever changed. The son who I loved deeply and who loved me beyond measure, who at one time brought only honor to our name, has in his darkest end, brought immeasurable shame and disgrace to this family. The likes I fear will bear bitter fruit for generations to come."

No one dared speak, but upon their faces she saw truth in her words. "I am worn down and devastated by Johnny's ruthless murder of the President. His actions have blackened us all. There is nothing more to be said."

The oak floorboards creaked as the matriarch made her way to her well-worn rocking chair near the hearth, a chair that had spent years in motion soothing the ten Booth children who were born to Junius and Mary Ann Booth. Sadly, only six children escaped the clutches of cholera and smallpox to achieve a healthy adulthood, another sorrow that assailed her heart.

Breaking the quiet circle around the room, it was Edwin who stepped forward to his mother, bending on his knee as to address her face to face. Her second oldest son was of medium stature, his distinguished features reminiscent of the Booth lineage with raven wavy hair, deepest black eyes, and marble white skin. His refined voice and precise diction honed from years of professionally working on the stage heralded Edwin as one of the most famous actors of his generation. Regrettably, the fame and notoriety he achieved meant nothing now as the family gathered together in the shadows of the once happy home. A family shamed and scrutinized for having born and loved their lost son and youngest brother, Johnny.

"Dearest Mother," said Edwin, reaching for her hands to offer comfort. "Words cannot describe what has befallen our family in recent months. Grief and sadness rips through our hearts knowing our Johnny will forever now be villainized as a murderer."

Mary Ann saw heartache in Edwin that matched her own. She stroked his cheek, staring into the blackness of his eyes normally so handsome and appealing, but tonight bore traces of suffering under the veil of shame and misery.

"Yes, is true. The Johnny we all adored is no more, leaving behind a monstrous legacy of hate and murder." Just saying it aloud caused her heart to clench. "Oh, what could have happened to our bright beautiful boy to cause him to commit such a crime?"

"Only Johnny and God above can answer that question," Edwin stated gently.

Mary Ann sighed deeply, reminiscing the past. "Remember that old gypsy who read his palm years ago, right here at Tudor Hall? She told us Johnny would become famous, love many, leave broken hearts, and die in a blaze of despair." She shook her head with that knowledge, the tattle of the old gypsy's words striking too true.

"Mother, I have something to tell you," Edwin said. There was a glimmer of hope in his voice as he glanced over his shoulder at his sister, Asia, who nodded in agreement. "We have news. Something that seemed so unbelievable to me, to us as a family. News I doubted at first, but Asia urged me to hear. I had to see it, understand for myself, to know it was true before we could bring you here in private to tell you."

"Oh Edwin," as she gripped his hands tight, hoping the news was the family was able to secure Johnny's body for his family to properly bury him. "I thought President Johnson was not releasing him, keeping our Johnny instead buried under the floorboards of the Old Federal Penitentiary in Washington, D.C. A miserable end of my beautiful and beloved son."

Hoping it was this news, Mary Ann rose from her rocking chair, pulling Edwin to stand. "Where is he? You brought me here, so I might gaze upon that handsome face one more time before oblivion takes me? Please take me to him. I must see him again, my son, my bright boy Absalom."

Edwin motioned toward Junius, who moved alongside their mother. Asia and Rosalie also stepped out of the shadows to surround the matriarch, stopping her from leaving.

"What is this?" She looked at the faces of her family, eldest son Junius so like his father and valiant brother Edwin who was the rock they all leaned upon. Rosalie, sweet and quietly devoted to her mother was fair and light, the only one of the Booth siblings to resemble Mary Ann's side of the family. Missing from the circle was youngest son Joe, who was away studying medicine at New York University.

And then her gaze fell upon Asia, a woman as beautiful as her brother John was handsome. Deep set, dark, intelligent eyes with a heart overflowing with compassion, even after bearing three sons she remained lovely of face and figure.

In their youth Asia and Johnny were especially close, both lovers of nature, poetry and art. The two were "thick like thieves," Mary Ann would often say to them both, for if one were lost, surely the other would follow.

These thoughts skated across her mind as she realized no one was speaking. They stepped back, exchanging peculiar glances that left her confused. Mary Ann once again asked of Edwin, "Son, have you brought me here in secret tonight so we can see our dear Johnny?"

Everyone remained silent, but a floorboard creaked on the far side of the darkened living room. The oak flooring squeaked again, almost as if a foot was interrupting its stillness. That was impossible as all the family was gathered next to her.

Heart racing, she stepped forward feeling drawn by an invisible force, moving past her family as she again heard the floor moving. She watched as the flames from the oil lamps winced in the damp summer night as if straining to give additional light in the shadowed room, flickering yet revealing nothing.

Again, the oak floor complained with the insistence of a foot upon it. Her voice trembled as she called out across the room, "Whose there? Come out, right now."

Slowly a shadow emerged from the darkness. The form and outline achingly familiar as she stared at the man now taking shape. She noticed the noble and handsome profile, the dark richness of his hair veiled by the depths of night. Taking slow cautious steps, he moved closer. Her eyes strained and her heart lurched in disbelief. A rich baritone voice echoed across the silent room, a voice familiar, one she had thought forever silenced with the finality of death.

"Mother," he whispered.

Her blood ran cold despite the warmth of the damp humid night, one hand clutched her throat in trying to speak, but she could not. No words felt possible as he moved out of the darkness and stood within plain sight of the Booth family matriarch.

"Mother, I am the reason that brings you here tonight."

Mary Ann's body shook in disbelief, both hands now instinctively reaching to embrace the one she loved most, the one who had caused such pain and disgrace, the one who now stood before her looking handsome and resplendent, a picture of perfection in health and life.

"Johnny, is really you?" She trembled in the tense stillness of those gathered in the room. Observing with her own eyes the vital young man that was her son lurched at her heart, as she blinked back the shock and disbelief of seeing him.

"What is going on, this cannot be," she cried, "You are dead!"

Mary Ann's voice gained strength as she shouted to her other family, "This is a trick. The government is trying to trick us with this fake look alike, trying to get us to admit our involvement so they can murder us all. We knew nothing of this. The last of the conspirators will hang soon and the vengeful government would like nothing more than to take us with them!"

"Mother, please listen. It is your son, Johnny," begged the young man. "This is no trick. I escaped the barn. Please, just let me tell you everything," he begged again.

The shadowed outline of the strikingly handsome man danced upon the wall nearest the hearth, the flame from the lamps illuminating the features of the hauntingly familiar face.

It was his voice, his heartfelt plea that gave her pause. The matriarch yearned to embrace the son who returned from the dead, yet she feared he wasn't real. He moved a bit closer, reaching into the collar of his white shirt. He pulled out a gold medal on a chain. Her eyes brightened in recognition.

"Look," he brought it into the light.

It was the Agnus Dei medallion, the Lamb of God image. "Yes, I know it well. Johnny wore it always, a gift from dear sister Asia."

But believing felt impossible. Her heart had already been broken by loss, her trust in humanity burned to ashes by the horror of her son's deeds. "No. You are an imposter. You could have another medal like the one my Johnny had."

The young man kept his gaze focused on the face of the woman whose happiness he had promised to keep. He leaned closer, bent his handsome face, pushing back a lock of hair from his head revealing a faint scar received in childhood. An injury received from friends who carelessly tossed rocks and shells and one had cut a line across his forehead. That day a frantic Mrs. Booth had rushed her bleeding son to their neighbor Mrs. Rogers, the local caregiver to all with an ailment or injury.

Mary Ann's fingers were shaking as she gently touched the scar, remembering the day it happened and how good he was when receiving stitches, never crying out in pain or fear. Her hands slid to caress his marble white cheeks, now lightly tanned from the summer. It only added to his handsome features. There was no mistaking him; it was her beloved son Johnny.

It was then the realization broke from Mary Ann like the wail of a lost soul crying out to the night, "My Johnny is alive. My God, how is it you have brought my son back from the dead?"

Johnny reached to embrace his shocked mother.

"I am so sorry, forgive me."

She looked up at him, all at once feeling horrified and angry over his deed, yet rejoicing in the life set before her. Her normal strong maternal presence prevailed. "Johnny, for the deed you have committed there is no forgiveness here on this earth. It is between you and your God. But for the life He has spared, I am forever grateful. As my child, I forgive you. But I just don't understand any of this. What has happened, my son?"

She touched him over and over, running her hands over his solid frame, feeling the life and strength in his vital strong body. Seeing her shock, John helped her back to the rocking chair by the empty hearth to rest there. He stood before her, his brothers and sisters moving to encircle in solidarity around him.

John felt humbled by their forgiveness and willingness to help him and Emma. They deserved a full explanation of his actions. He drew a deep breath, explaining, "As a valued member of the Knights of the Golden Circle, I was sought out by leaders who claimed I alone could save the South. They choose me due to my fame, my ease into all society, my well-known disgust of the President, and the fact I thought he was a tyrant. I believed I would save the South and be revered as doing so. I was wrong."

"Yes, son. How terribly wrong you were!"

"I am not evil, Mother. But I was mistaken. I truly thought it would help my beloved South. It was all for nothing."

Johnny took a deep breath before he continued his voice firm and deliberate. "The man at Garrett's Farm who actually died was James W. Boyd, a fellow member of the Knights of the Golden Circle. He was a Confederate soldier and a spy. He heard though fellow operatives the New York Cavalry were closing in on Davy Herold and I, and had come to find us, then beaconed me to make haste and escape, with no time to spare."

"What happened then?"

"I escaped, while he stayed, trying to use his presence to divert the Calvary. But that too, failed. Boyd died in vain, shot in that barn along with all hope for victory. I was told I would be a hero, could avenge my beloved south by eliminating the leader of the Union and his cabinet. In this way, by decapitating the government, our southern forces could seize the day and rise again."

"But that was not true," she grieved, "None of it was."

John nodded, agreeing. "For this and all I have wrought, I am so very remorseful."

"As well you should be," but her heart had softened. "Where have you been hiding all these months?"

"I stumbled and crawled through that forest for a few days, alone and wounded. My compass was gone; my broken leg caused great pain. I had no idea where I was, no one to guide me, no help and no hope. I found a dead confederate, one of the bodies still strewn across the countryside with no one to claim or bury him. I switched clothes, taking his. The name Singer was embroidered on his cuff. I proceeded to a road where I eventually fell unconscious."

"An ambulance wagon found me, took me to the hospital in Alexandria, VA where I was called John Singer, as that was the name on the uniform. I had contracted malaria, but I was willed back to life and after recovering thinking and praying perhaps I could hide in plain sight."

Mary Ann looked at her son and asked quizzically, "Johnny what do you mean willed back to life?"

"If it were not for a kind and compassionate caregiver at the hospital, I would not be here. I believed my life should have been over, especially after the deed I committed, but God had other plans for me." With that statement John extended his hand and beaconed with his fingers toward the back of the shadowed room where he had been previously standing. The oak floors creaked as someone else moved over them. The faint sounds of footsteps resonated in the tense silence.

Mary Ann waited. In the candlelight illuminating her loved ones, a beautiful blonde woman stepped forward to stand beside her son. Her hand nervously reached for John's and held it fast to her side. She noticed quickly the fairness of her face, perfect proportions and lightness of eyes. She was exquisite.

"Mother, this is Emma. She took care of me, brought me back to life from injury and illness. By the grace of her love, she gave me back the will to live." He swallowed, glanced at Emma before continuing. "We were married at her parents' home in Richmond this past May."

"What you are married?"

"Yes, mother. I love Emma. She owns my heart."

John sternly cautioned her as he said, "We go by the name of Singer, for the world believes John Wilkes Booth is dead and buried. And so, it must stay this way. But his is my wife, Mrs. John Singer." He smiled at the lovely blonde, leaned his head and placed a light kiss upon her brow.

Mary Ann could see in their faces the love her son had found. It was around them, it was in them, a tangible bond no one who saw them together could deny. Rising from the rocking chair where the shock of seeing her son alive had sent her, she extended her quivering hand to her new daughter-in-law and said gently, "Come closer, child. Let me see you, how beautiful you are."

Emma grasped her hand and said, "Mother Booth, I love your son John very much. Since the day he first looked at me in the hospital I knew there would be no other man for me, ever."

Mary Ann assessed Emma, noticing for the first time the tight surgeons wrap around her shoulder. "You are injured."

Although pale and clearly in discomfort, Emma said in an uplifted voice, "Yes, there was an incident at my family's home in

Richmond. But we were fortunate. John is safe. And with rest and care the shoulder will heal, in time."

"I can see you adore him."

"I do, with all my heart."

"And you know his truths?" Mary Ann questioned, "You married my son without pretense or doubt of his identity?"

"Yes, I went to the altar vowing before God that my name from henceforth is Mrs. John Singer, yet I knew all along that I was marrying John Wilkes Booth." Emma hesitated and looked at her husband for permission, who nodded, urging her to continue, "In fact, I knew his identity before we married, as I found a small red date book in his disposed military uniform. Inside he had saved news clippings about the assassination, along with a personal letter written by John, addressed to Asia Booth Clarke in Philadelphia."

"I never told John I knew of his deception until after our marriage. Although he felt determined to remain hidden as John Singer to protect everyone, I felt his family deserved to know he had survived. Days after we married, in secret I traveled to Philadelphia to deliver the letter to Asia and to let her know, her brother John was not only alive, but had found love and was married to me. I begged her to come with me, to see him."

Mary Ann's expression was frozen in disbelief. His incredible survival was against all odds, and her Johnny finding real love was just too unbelievable to comprehend. With suspicion, she narrowed her eyes at Emma, unwilling to blindly trust this newcomer. "How could you possibly persuade Asia to leave her house, her small boys and infant son with just the evidence of a letter? It could have been a fake or a fraud! Asia's husband and brothers Junius and Edwin had been imprisoned in Washington." The bitterness she harbored for John's sins could not be contained. "Their only crime was being family to the assassin of the President!"

Asia stepped beside Emma in solidarity. "Mother," she gently explained, "Emma was incredibly brave to do what she did."

Mary Ann listened.

"Emma came not knowing anything of me or of our family, putting her life at risk if the proof she held had been found. Yet, determined to unite our family, she alone travelled the long and difficult rails from the devastated city of Richmond all the way to Philadelphia. And yes, convinced me she was telling the truth."

Mary Ann then asked of her daughter Asia, "Your family was imprisoned and you had a Federal guard in your home for several weeks after your brother's terrible deed, so daughter, tell me, by what device did Emma convince you?"

Johnny added to Emma's tale, "It was her description of the Agnus Dei, undeniable proof to Asia this was true. The letter I had penned was written on April 25. The words were undoubtedly mine. I was desperate when I wrote it. In the letter, I said goodbye."

The gold medallion still lay in view around his neck. Asia had put it there the year prior, when the angel of death nearly stole John's life due to an accident on stage. This proof was a certainty. The eyes of the matriarch teared in remembrance of the death watch that was graced to pass by her beloved Johnny.

"Emma told Asia of the medal, described it and delivered the letter. I had written it while on the run with Davey Herold, the night we crossed the Rappahannock River. I thought the red diary and its contents were lost in my transport to the hospital and or burned after I contracted malaria, but I later learned Emma had found it. I had no idea Emma knew my secrets. I intended to continue living as John Singer, feeling living a ruse was better than Emma knowing the truth."

"Yet, she knew."

"Yes. I fell in love with Emma, could not believe I was given the second chance to live and love again."

The lovely blonde woman smiled at John, showing her joy at his heartfelt words.

John then continued, "Upon Emma's return to Richmond, I saw the carriage approach the house. I ran to the garden to greet my bride with a bouquet. Emma had claimed she was visiting an ill friend in Philadelphia, but it was not true as I found her in the drawing room and with her our beloved Asia. "

"And then you told Edwin and Rosalie," the Booth matriarch rightly assumed.

"Yes. We all arrived here to Tudor Hall, traveling under the cover of night. "Mother," continued John, "I know this is truly shocking news to you and to the family gathered here but there is more and I need help."

"For although the government believes they have their man, dead and buried, there are still those who saw me at the hospital who believe I am not Singer. Their eyes have seen my diary. There are men after me now, one whose hysteria has bred doubt. I must make haste to leave, to escape across this nation or possibly too far off lands. Only by disappearing can I be sure of your safety, especially now that you all know I am alive."

No one seemed to deny the knowledge that by surviving, John put the whole family in danger.

"I ask of you, my family, to take to your heart my dear beloved wife whose love I do not deserve yet have embraced from the moment I saw her beautiful face. Please help me escape, and take care of my Emma until such time, if ever, it is safe for her to join me."

A grasp resonated through the room from Emma; she whirled to face her husband. "What say you, John?" Obviously, she had not known his future plans. "Wherever you go I shall go. I cannot be parted from you. Please darling, my heart will forever be broken. You are not to be parted from me, or our child."

"Emma," replied John, "I cannot take you unto my flight, for you know men believe I am an imposter, who blame me for the shooting in the barn in Richmond. You know Henry Bradley will hunt me down, try to kill me. I cannot have you with me on this life," he softened his tone as he reached his hand to Emma's stomach, where the promise of a child was growing. "I need to know you are safe and well, our love bringing forth our child."

Emma fell into John's arms, her sobbing echoing through the large room. Asia stepped forth and took Emma to sit upon the sofa and went to bring the expectant mother a soothing draught to settle her down.

The distraught family stood gasping as the news of an expectant child cut through the room. The thought of how to keep John and Emma safe raced through their minds.

"My God, my God" murmured Mary Ann as the news began to sink in, "A child is coming, my Johnny's child. God help us. It is a child born of tragedy."

The family stared at one another in ghastly silence. The only sound came from the faint drum of rain that had begun to fall upon the tin roof of Tudor Hall and the muffled sobbing of Emma being comforted by Asia.

It was brother Edwin who finally dispelled the shock. He strode forward to face his wayward brother. With a strong angry voice said to him, "My bright boy, my Absalom," His lips were tight as he repeated the same again, "My bright boy, my Absalom."

John could not look at Edwin who was justifiably revolted by his actions, needing to express the agony and shame he and the family endured because of John's crime.

"You know that story well, don't you Johnny?" Edwin spat.

"Yes, that is right from the Bible." He swallowed, finally meeting his eyes. "Absalom was King David's third and most favored son. That son later died tragically, but not before he murdered his own half-brother, and set about to steal his father's reign."

"You are the third Booth son Johnny. Was this biblical lesson in your mind?"

"No brother it was not!"

Edwin clicked his tongue in a sound of disapproval, "And yet you as the favored son and sibling could commit this evil and lay our family in the path of danger. You have shamed us. We have grieved and felt broken hearted to the point of death, ourselves. Now you dare come to us now, back from a certain death with a wife and child, no less. You defy all right and reason, brother."

"I'm a truly sorry."

Edwin simply held up his palm, stopping John from speaking. "Asia already explained to me your need to find passage away from here. I can see from Emma's injured shoulder there is truth in the fact certain men doubt your pseudo as John Singer and seek to find and destroy you. It appears once again, someone else paid for your sins."

John's jaw dropped; he started to object.

"Before you speak, just know that as your brother I have done my duty. A place of refuge has already been secured for you and Emma. With that said, Johnny, you will leave Tudor Hall tomorrow, as the danger that swills about here is palpable. I have arranged a small farmhouse in the Shenandoah Valley, in Martinsburg. You will travel directly there. Do not return."

"Thank you."

"More than this I cannot say." Edwin still fumed, "I am beyond words. Look to our dear mother for forgiveness. Although your family will do the right thing and see to your safety and ensure Emma's well-being, it is God who will judge you. Not I. Not us."

With those words denouncing his brother's actions, Edwin walked away to stand in his previous place between Junius and Rosalie. Still frustrated, Edwin signed and ran his hands through dark long wavy hair, his jet-black eyes reflective of the intense Booth family traits, all the while staring at Johnny waiting for an explanation that could never change the course of history.

John stood silent, his eyes on the shadowy floor, unable to find the apology that he knew would change nothing. He realized as he looked upon the grieving faces of his family that repenting of his crime would never be enough. He would pay, both in this life and in whatever came after. God would indeed judge him. As he lifted his head to speak, it was his mother Mary Ann who filled his sight line, the one to whom he had promised that he would see to it that her happiness would always come first. And now he realized how horribly he had failed at that promise.

With the family about her in support, Mary Ann seemed to have accepted his marriage and the fact he was still alive, but was determined to say her piece and share with her son exactly what happened to the family, as each member heard of the horrible news on that horrible day. "Johnny my son," she began quietly, "You are alive and you cannot know the joy of seeing you now.

But that terrible day the newsboys were crying out, the President's death was by the hands of John Wilkes Booth. When this horrid news affronted me I cried out in my deepest agony, * "O God, if this be true, let him shoot himself, let him not live to be hung ! Spare him, spare us, and spare the name that dreadful disgrace!' Then in the midst of this news, the postman's whistle rang to the door and brought a letter to me written by you, see, see here?"

John watched as his mother pulled out from the pocket in the skirt of her dress a folded letter, the scrawl on the envelope familiar. She began to read the haunting words to the family.

> **To Mary Ann Holmes Booth*
> *Washington, D.C. 14 April 1865*
> *April 14, 2 A.M.*
>
> *Dearest Mother:*
> *I know you expect a letter from me, and am sure you will*
> *hardly forgive me. But indeed, I have nothing to write about.*
> *Everything is dull; that is, has been till last night. (The*
> *Illumination.)*
> *Everything was bright and splendid. More so if it had been*
> *a display in a nobler cause. But so goes the world. Might*
> *makes right. I only drop you these few lines to let you know I*
> *am well, and to say I have not heard from you. Excuse*
> *brevity; am in haste. Had one from Rose. With best love to*
> *you all, I am your affectionate son ever,*
> *John*

"Son," she sadly said, "How could you? Can you not imagine what reading this letter did to my heart? In the hours before committing your terrible crime you wrote this letter to me as if nothing unusual was going on. Yet soon afterward your actions would bring such overwhelming sorrow, a cloud of misery to our family. I cannot understand this. Yet, you have explained tonight how you were supplanted in the barn by a fellow confederate operative and were able to escape. You claim you were the "tool" of other men. But I don't understand."

John held his mother's hands and took them to his cheek, feeling warmth and love from the woman that he so adored. "Mother, it is true. I was the "tool" of other men, my fame, my money, my ease into all society helped in this cause by the Knights of the Round Table. It has all come apart. I am unable to find those who were my aides. But, until such time, I am John Singer now."

Mary Ann shook her head as if by doing so could dispel the pallor of grief in the silent room. She shuffled her feet to stand nearest her daughter Asia who sat on the sofa holding John's wife. She touched the shoulder of her new daughter in law.

"Dearest God," she prayed quietly, "This innocent young woman, now married to my son, is carrying my next grandchild. Protect them and this family from the tragedy that I fear, most certainly lies ahead."

Asia rose from her seat next to Emma, allowing her mother to sit beside the distraught young woman who was still struggling with the news that John perhaps intended to leave without her.

It was to Asia to tell John all of what happened to the family the day, the hour, the moment his crime came to them, as the grim reaper tried to come to claim its next victim.

"Johnny" began Asia, "Although there is nothing now or ever that will change the past few months, we can learn from this and we can change the outcome. You must know of the terrible pain and suffering you caused."

"Yes, sister. I am aware."

"You have Emma to consider and care for. You must think clearly, without rash impulsive moves that injure others. Throughout our lives we have rose above hardship, above our father's betrayals that could have labeled us as bastards. Even after he and Mother married, we stayed strong because we were a FAMILY. Here and now tonight with your family, we will remain a united front. And, dearest brother, know it is united but with an uncertain future."

"I'm trying to make amends, Asia."

"How, by leaving Emma and thinking only of yourself?"

John felt offended, "My only thought is for her safety. It is not my intention to be unkind to her or my family right now."

"Oh, but you are. Your personal need for vengeance against the President and to become a hero became far more important to you that caring for the people who you claim to love and who love you."

He hung his head, feeling truth in her words.

"Can you even fathom how I felt? I was in Philadelphia that morning with the headlines of the day screaming the most grievous news! There I was expectant with child and resting in bed, hysterical beyond words. Then, without warning, my husband John Sleeper was arrested. For your crimes! Junius was at work, acting in Cincinnati. He came to our house to comfort me, and he too was arrested. Both men were completely innocent. Yet were hauled off to the Old Capital Prison in Washington, questioned relentlessly about you and were treated like criminals. Our younger brother Joseph was just back from Australia, but he too was arrested before landing in New York City. Thanks to his influential friends, Edwin was helped to alleviate that event;

however he was followed with a guard of spies to watch his every moment."

He had not known the extent of their persecution. It filled his soul with a pit of shame.

"Arrests happened to the most innocent of people with no affiliations to your political addenda. There were no reasons, no warnings, with neighbors and friends suddenly being suspicious of our wrongdoing, purely by association with you. We were humiliated and ostracized beyond reason, cast aside with prejudice where none before existed."

"And did you consider our poor mother? She heard the news from a newsboy in the streets calling the name Booth as the assassin and murderer, in the same rant. You were driven to commit this heinous crime, without thought or regard as to how your actions would affect us. Now that fateful day and your unforgivable crime have brought us here under the cover of night. We are seen as being complicit in your crime. But we are guilty of nothing more than being your family."

"I am eternally sorry, Asia. I was blind."

"I do love you. But you had to hear the truth." Asia reached for John's hand and held out her other hand toward the members of the Booth family. She waited as brothers Junius, and Edwin and sister Rosalie joined them, standing around in solidarity.

It was only when the presence of Emma was added that their unity was confirmed, as the future of the small family hiding in plain sight hung in a fearful balance of uncertainty.

CHAPTER TWO

Tudor Hall in Bel Air, Maryland

"Johnny, show yourself, you have nothing to fear from me!"
~~ Mrs. Elijah Rogers

It was a knock upon the front door that sent the Booth family into a panic. No one, no neighbor and no other relative knew of their secret nighttime visit to the family home.

From behind the door an old yet familiar voice resonated across the threshold, "Who is there? Open the door."

The knock became more frantic. The family was frozen in fear when Edwin stepped past them as they gathered by the hearth. "Johnny, Emma," he quietly demanded, "Fall back into the shadows, now. Hide yourselves quickly."

With that John gathered his wife to his side and stood in the shadow of the room, far away from the flickering lamps. He held her tight trying to shield her from the intruder. His heart sank as he realized their future life together would be similar to this very moment, hiding in the shadows forever, fearful of a simple knock at the door.

"Open the door, right this moment!" The female voice demanded. "Who is inside that house?"

The knocking continued until Edwin finally strode to the door and opened it. His eyes befell upon the matronly countenance of their long time neighbor, Mrs. Rogers.

"Edwin," she cried out in relief, "I am so glad it is you."

"Hello, Mrs. Rogers."

"I feared intruders had taken over your home. I have taken it upon myself to pass by the house since that fateful night all of you fled and I was shocked to see a light from the road. How it is you have come back to Tudor Hall?"

Being familiar with the home, Mrs. Rogers made her way past the front hall nearest the hearth where she had spent many happy times visiting Mary Ann, watching her brood of children grow as the family filled the grounds of Tudor Hall with their laughter and antics.

She then paused long enough to notice the family standing awkwardly about the room. No one stepped forward to greet her, as if a stranger had darkened their doorway.

She saw Mary Ann and sighed with relief, "Oh my dearest friend, I am so glad to see you. How my heart has been grief stricken with worry for your family. But why did you not wire me to tell me you were all coming? I would have prepared your home, had foodstuffs ready, linens clean and fresh for the bedding."

She stood in the middle of the room wringing her hands, no one speaking and no one moving. Their fear in the moment of discovery had turned the family to ice, unable to move or think.

"What is going on here," she inquired, "Mary Ann, Edwin, all you Booths know me. I helped bring forth most of you children. What is amiss?"

The family exchanged odd looks.

It was Mrs. Rogers herself who shouted to the family, "I knew it! He's alive, isn't he? I have felt it all along. I have loved that boy since the day I saw him, love him still, even with this heinous deed to darken his soul."

The room stayed silent.

"Johnny," she cried out into the darkness, "If you are here, show yourself, son, you have nothing to fear from me."

The floorboards then creaked as the shadow moved from the darkness nearest the lamps and John stood before the old neighbor.

Her hand flew to cover her heart as she cried out, "You're alive, you're alive! I knew you would somehow escape."

Her hands were shaking as she reached for him, caressing his face and stopping at his forehead to feel the scar from the wound she had bound for him as a small boy, a silent validation of his identity.

"Johnny my boy," she explained, "That terrible night I readied a ham and bread for you and placed a lamp light in my window, for if your escape brought you through here, my light would let know you I would help you."

Stepping back from John she turned to the Booth family, stunned by the genuine love of their longtime neighbor.

"Mary Ann, children, I have known you all since coming to Tudor Hall. I have helped to bring forth some of you here as well as buried members of your family here as well. You have nothing to fear from me. Your secret will be as safe as between blood. Nothing seen or done here shall ever be repeated, ever."

But John remained adamant, "Mrs. Rogers, this night you have seen me is to be forgotten. There are those who do not believe in my ruse and I believe are at this very moment looking for me. This stop at Tudor Hall was to tell Mother that I was alive and to ask the aid of my family to help me find safety somewhere."

The elderly neighbor noticed an unknown woman on the sofa and her eyes widened.

"For you see," John continued, "it is not just me that I must care for. I am married. My wife must above all else be protected and safe. She has been through so much and she pregnant with my child."

A light weeping was heard across the room as Asia comforted her sister-in-law. It was a lot for Emma, the traveling, the healing shoulder wound and her pregnancy. The weakened state was overwhelming for the young bride.

Mrs. Rogers stepped towards Asia, whom she saw comforting the hunched form of a young woman.

Emma heard the old neighbor ask of her, "Do not weep. Tell me your name, and where are you from?"

Emma's chin quivered as she replied to the old neighbor, "My name is Emma. I am from Richmond. My father and brother were killed in the first battle of Manassas. Our home during the war was next to the White House of the Confederacy, used by Jeff Davis and his Presidency in the Confederate Capitol. It was after my father and brother were killed that I travelled to an Alexandria Field Hospital to help our soldiers in whatever way I could. I stayed there for three years. It was the last group of soldiers that came in from the ambulance, I saw John. I saw him and never looked back."

Mrs. Rogers placed her hand under Emma chin to fully gaze upon her beautiful face. The old neighbor studied the young bride and resounded her prophecy to the family, "A beauty you have here, Johnny." She smiled and said, "Your children will be light of hair like their mother, but with the dark smoldering eyes of the Booth's."

Emma grasped the woman's hand and smiled. Mrs. Rogers then heard the faint cry of an infant from upstairs. She watched as Asia rushed up the hardwood stairs to the second floor of Tudor Hall, hurrying to soothe the infant cries.

John drew the attention of the old neighbor again.

"My dearest Mrs. Rogers, seeing you again has been good. My youth comes to light in remembrance of my childhood visits to your farm and the warm welcoming smells from your kitchen. Stopping there on Sunday's on my way to church with dear sister Rosalie was always a treat. I can still smell the fresh baked bread and jams."

"Ah yes," she smiled, her eyes gleaming, "you were always welcome, like a son you are to me. This seems so unreal. Although my heart knew, I cannot believe my own eyes you are alive."

The reunion between neighbors was interrupted as the sound of footsteps coming back down the stairs. Asia was returning with her infant John Joseph in her arms. But she was accompanied by a young child who followed behind; they could hear his petulant sleepy voice complaining to his mother, "John Joseph cryin' woke me. Mama, it's dark. I want to go back to sleep."

John stood quiet as he watched his sister appear with her infant in her arms. In the lamplight, he could see his nephew Jacob in his white sleeping shirt. The small boy was dragging the toy horse John had gifted to the boys on his last visit to Philadelphia.

Apparently, Joshua was still fast asleep upstairs, undisturbed by the cries of his infant brother.

Emma stepped forward to sooth and help Asia, who had her hands full with the baby. She knelt down to greet the unhappy boy. "Jacob, do you remember me? I am Emma, remember I came to your house?"

Jacob wiped the sleep from his dark eyes, his face and youthful features so like his Uncle's John's.

"You're so pretty." He blinked, waking more as he looked at Emma. "I remember. You came to our house. I showed you my toy horse. Mama told me I had to be a big boy for Joshua and John Joseph and not to tell anyone she was leaving with you, but I cried some."

"I'm so very sorry, Jacob."

"See," he began, "One night I could not sleep, and I thought I heard Uncle John telling us he was alive, to come find him. Mama told me she heard his voice too. Then a few days later, she left with you." The young boy being inquisitive could hold his tongue no longer, "Is everyone still mad at Uncle John?'

Emma rose from her slightly bent position.

Jacob looked past her to notice the figures of this grandmother and aunts and uncles in the Tudor Hall family room. He was always happy to be spoiled by them all, but there was one person in particular whose presence drew him immediately.

"Uncle John!"

The screams of joy from within an innocent child's heart pierced the room with exquisite love and delight. The boy's chubby legs took off running, his arms outstretched as if John would disappear if he did not reach him.

"Jacob my boy, come here!" cried John.

The boy leapt into his arms. They surrounded the boy completely and held him tight, bound by the deep love and heartfelt connection the two shared. They squeezed and held each other, crying and kissing each other's faces.

"Jacob, my beautiful nephew." Tears wet John's cheeks, unchecked. "I love you, child. Oh, heart of my heart. I have missed you so."

Jacob snuggled into his Uncle's neck, small arms wrapped around the man who from the moment of his birth held a unique and special bond.

"Uncle John," the excited cries came from the young boy, "I asked Mama when she left with Emma to go find you and she did, she did! I have missed you!" He drew back to look his uncle in the eyes,

"Why are people saying bad things about you? I don't believe
them I just don't!"

The little boy pointed his chin in the air with a dramatic flair
so reminiscent of his theatrical family members. At a loss for
words, John gently put him down. He picked up the toy horse
that had dropped as they hugged, kneeling to return it into
Jacob's chubby hand.

"Child, how brave you have been for your mother and younger
brothers. I know how proud she is of you and how very much she
loves you. You've been a big boy while I've been gone."

Jacob beamed with joy and cast his bright innocent smile at
Emma, "Thank you for coming to my house that day. You brought
back Uncle John. I'm so happy. I love you too." The young boy
lowered his head and dropped his eyes, the black satin eyelashes
wet with sudden tears.

Emma responded, "Jacob, I love you too."

Immediately his gaze met hers and a wide smile crossed his
sweet face.

"Of course, child. We are family now. You know Uncle John
and I are married." He nodded and continued to smile. "At
Christmas time I hope to give your Uncle a beautiful boy just like
you, and he will be your cousin."

Jacob had no time to answer Emma as a voice from the other
side of the room called to him.

"Jacob," a voice called. "Come over here. I want to talk to you."
John sat in an armchair near Mary Ann who rested again in the
rocking chair nearest oil lamps over the cold hearth. He picked
up Jacob to settle him upon his knee.

"My sweetest boy, you are smart beyond your years. You asked
if people were still angry with me. I must tell you, yes, some are.
You must have seen and heard many things these past months."
Jacob nodded adamantly. "You must know how very much I love
you. Don't be afraid. Be brave and speak the truth. Please, tell me
what happened the day the soldiers came and took your daddy
away?"

The young boy's lower lip quivered as he boldly faced John.
The eyes reflecting back were exactly like his Uncle's, black,
bottomless and compelling.

"Well," began Jacob, "It was morning. Me and Joshua was
playing in the front parlor by the fireplace. Daddy was home and
Mama was in the kitchen helping Mrs. McLeary with breakfast.
All of sudden we heard horses riding hard to the front door. Then
soldiers were pounding on it. They ran in the house and started
pushing Daddy, saying things 'bout someone killing the
President. He fell and the soldiers kicked him some. I was
crying."

"I am so sorry Jacob." "Go on."

"They tied up Daddy's hands and the soldiers started messing up the house. They took a bunch of papers and burned some in the fireplace. They found the place in the wall where Daddy has stuff. They pointed a big gun at him until he told them how to open it. That made the soldiers mad."

"Where was your Mama?"

"Oh, I think she ran upstairs. I remember she came back, yelling at the men to leave. She had the locket with your picture in it. She wore it around her neck. The soldiers tried to take it, but Mama cried so much over it the soldiers left it. We thought Mama was going away with the soldiers, but she could not leave me and Joshua, plus she was waiting for John Joseph to be born."

John glanced across the room at his sister, who was nursing the infant and felt the weight of their reality heavy on his heart.

"The soldiers shoved Daddy out of the house and took him away. Poor Mama she fell down to the ground crying and crying. She was so sad cause of the stuff the soldiers said you did, Uncle John. I don't understand, it was so awful. Our friends that Joshua and I used to play with stopped coming into our yard, and Mama wouldn't let us out to play. It's been like that, always now. Did you really do something bad? Is that why everyone is mad at you?"

John looked into the eyes of his most favored nephew and sighed deeply. "Yes, son. I did do something very bad, and I am very sorry for it. And I cannot change it back or ever make it better. Do you understand?"

"I am not sure." His brow puckered with thought, "But we are all here together and we can be a family again, right?"

"Jacob," his mother Asia called to him, "That is enough for now. Come, it's time for bed."

"No Asia," interrupted John, "I will take him to bed, like I used to Ready, Jacob?"

The boy sprang into action, the serious moments forgotten. He climbed onto his Uncle's back. As they galloped up the stairs, the delightful sounds of Jacob's laughter and glee cut the decisive pallor of sadness from the room.

John ran up the stairs, the sounds and feeling of the hardwood familiar and comfortable under his boots. He stopped to peer out the window on the landing, noticing the moonrise starting its night's journey in the evening sky. How many times he had climbed these very stairs, going to the room at the top of the staircase, directly left of the one that faced east?

In the bedroom, an oil lamp had been lit by Asia. John moved the boy from his shoulders and carried him to the mattress, careful of the sleeping boy Joshua, the middle boy. John moved the quilt down to cover his nephew, even though it was a humid night. The blanket brought comfort from the night air, which might disturb a child's sleep. He noticed the details on the handmade quilt, the one of Job from the Bible. His sister Asia had made it for him as a young man. He sighed as he pulled up the covers, preparing to tuck in the boy he loved so much.

"You must try to sleep so you can be strong and good for your mother."

"Yes, I will. When I wake up you won't be gone will you, Uncle John? Mama has been so sad since the soldiers came. Can't it be like it was before? Everyone will be happy you are back."

John gathered up his nephew and hugged the boy to him. "Nothing will ever be same. But one thing you must always carry in your heart is my love for you. I love you now and until the day I die, you are very precious to me."

Jacob quietly sobbed at his Uncle's words as John rested him back upon the pillow. He wiped the tears away from the young noble handsome face and stroked his cheek.

"Sleep now, not to worry. I promise to be here when you wake up."

John waited beside Jacob a few moments more until the sound of the child breathing came soft and even, like the faint fluttering of angel's wings.

He rose, walked the familiar path across the room toward the floor to ceiling Tudor doors that led outside to his Romeo and Juliet balcony. Many a day and night as a young man had been spent on that balcony practicing his Shakespeare and honing his voice as a finely tuned theatrical instrument.

With an aching nostalgic in his heart, he opened the doors and stepped outside. From his vantage point facing east, he could see the barn in the moonlight. The woods beyond were a favorite place, where he often rode his horse Cola. They would wander and gallop for hours. The memories at that moment felt overwhelming, remembering himself as playing Romeo to his lovely sister Asia as Juliet. Moments frozen in time, never to come again.

Wiped away forever now by his one heinous act.

He turned away from the memories, then stepped back into the room and once again gazed upon the sleeping boys. So innocent and pure. He prayed they would remain safe.

Returning downstairs, John was back in the midst of his family. His heart was heavy. All eyes turned to look, some expectant, others gleaming with emotions.

In silence he walked to his sister Asia, took her hand and kissed it. Her eyes filled with tears as the pain of their reality took hold.

"Dearest sister mine, seeing those boys upstairs as innocent as angels, their hearts so pure and loving is humbling. What have I done to deserve their love? Nothing. I stand before you riddled by guilt and a heart that is barely alive, if only by the grace of my beautiful wife. The pain I heard and saw in Jacob has torn into me. I realize perhaps it would truly have been better if I had died in that barn. To be living is surely worse now than death. How do I go on, having stained the heart of that beautiful boy who still declares his love for me?"

"Johnny," whispered Asia, "What is done cannot be undone. We can only move forward with what we have been given and that is your life. No matter what happens we are grateful that your life has been spared. Your family will not leave you. We will only protect you."

Emma approached Asia and John, the exhaustion of the night's events etched upon her lovely face. She reached for her husband and said to him "John, perhaps this child will be a boy like Jacob, a son that will give you great joy husband; it is what I have prayed for."

John turned and faced his wife; he placed his hand lightly on the sides of her stomach and smiled.

"Dearest wife, it is my greatest plea to God that this child not only be healthy, but I pray will also be a girl. One like you so I may spoil her from her infancy. She will not only be beautiful, but so very loved. Our very own Juliet."

John reached for Emma then and wholly embraced her, his arms covering her, protecting both mother and child.

Edwin stood silent across the room, overwhelmed by so much emotion. His anger at John still burned, but he would do whatever was right. The hour was late and the decision for John and Emma to leave was fast approaching. The life and safety off all his family was all he could think about.

"John, I think it's best to get the women off to rest," said Edwin. "Mother please go with Mrs. Rogers for the night. Rosalie and Junius will go with you. We were blessed she appeared tonight, as her home is ready and comfortable for you. Tudor Hall is but a shadow of its former self. The company and assurance from an old and dearest friend would be best right now."

"Yes, Mary Ann," Mrs. Rogers added, "Let's return to the comfort and warmth of my home. Tomorrow will be here soon enough."

Mary Ann walked over to John while he had been embracing Emma. She tenderly reached to touch him again as if still unbelieving he was truly alive.

"Do not leave without saying goodbye, my son," Mary Ann whispered to him.

"Mother, please go with Mrs. Rogers. I will be here in the morning I promise." He bent over and kissed her brow, holding her hand to his cheek before releasing it.

Once the other family members had departed, Edwin addressed Asia, Emma, and John. His shoulders were weighted with the responsibility of protecting his family.

"There is much to talk about, many decisions to bear to mind for you and your family, and for all of us as well. But the night is long, and it is best to rest now. We will act decisively in the morning. By some miracle or fate you are alive, and I vow that you shall stay alive. Asia was right, our family will see to it."

John felt humbled, "Your help is more that I deserve, especially after everything I have done to this family and to tarnish the Booth name."

"Repent then to God, Johnny," admonished Edwin. "Only the deity above can help your soul. Your earthly life and physical safety are what your family will see to. Good night, brother."

With that Edwin turned away quickly, disappearing into the shadowy house. They heard his footsteps climb the steps to the second-floor bedrooms, to the one located past John's on the left.

Asia also prepared to leave. "You may use the bedroom shared by Rosalie and I, as girls. I have prepared the bed with fresh linens. As you saw, the boys and I are in your old room." She sighed, stopping at the foot of the stairs.

"Johnny," she reminisced, "The room I take my rest, where my children slumber is one I remember so very well. The balcony, the uncarpeted floors, the books, the straw mattress with my quilt. That bedroom faces east. You said you wanted that room as to greet each and every day, not wanting to watch it wane into the gloom of night. Do you remember?"

"Yes, I do."

Tears slid down her cheeks. "Goodnight. It is good we have this one last night together, under the same roof where we were once so young and happy at heart. For tomorrow, the world awaits."

John and Emma watched as Asia ascended the stairs. They stood alone in the empty living room, with only the two lighted lamps on the mantle interrupting the darkness shrouding the cottage. Emma leaned her head on her husband's shoulder resting there as his arms held her. John stroked her golden hair, his heart weary and aching.

"I beg you now to tell me again you love me," he begged Emma, "Quickly, for here in the midst of my family with the pain and heartbreak I see on their faces; I know I am unworthy of such devotion and love, not only from them but from you, dearest wife. If you had not willed me back to life through the sweltering fever of malaria, I might now be at the gates of hell, for surely that is where I belong, to burn forever without end for all I have done and all the agony that I have wrought."

Emma lifted her head, the tears streaming down her lovely face. John smoothed the wet marks from her silken cheeks.

"I love you John. There will never be anyone else for me. This child, our child is proof of our love. Yes, what has been done cannot be undone. Where we are now is our life to live. You have been given a second chance to live and love again. We must go forth in this life together. Do not ever dare to say you will leave me, again."

"If that is your wish," cooed John.

"Darlin,' as it is only your love that has kept breath within my body. I will speak to Edwin in the morning about the home he has located a home for us in the Shenandoah. A home for us, for you and you and our Juliet."

He smiled as he said the name of their child.

Emma sighed deeply as exhaustion began to claim her. "If it is a girl yes. But I am curious why you have proposed the name of Juliet? It is nothing we had discussed before."

"When I was upstairs in my old room, putting that sweet boy Jacob to sleep, the balcony called to me. I slipped quietly through the doors and looked around at a view I have loved my whole life, one that is blazed into my memory. In my memories, I could still hear far away voices of myself and Asia in our youth, practicing the lines from one of my favorite Shakespearean plays, Romeo and Juliet. I thought it would be perfect name."

"Because it is from a play you love?" Emma asked innocently.

John considered all that had transpired, events and mistakes that brought them to this night. "No, it's because Juliet is a child born from tragedy."

He then walked over to the mantle and put out the lamps on either end. As they made their way to the stairs, the moon had just sliced through the night clouds, shining a silvery path around them that gleamed through the Tudor window on the landing. It seemed a sign, as to deliver them safety and rest.

CHAPTER THREE

Tudor Hall in Bel Air, Maryland

"You are here Uncle John, you are really here."
~~ Jacob Junius Booth Clarke

It seemed as John had just closed his eyes to sleep when movement outside his door awakened him fully. His blood froze with fear. Someone was outside their bedroom door. The thump that woke him sounded again. Careful not to wake Emma he rose from his bed, quickly yanked on clothes, and opened the door slightly.

He breathed in relief to see a small boy with dark hair and even darker eyes waiting in the hallway. It was Jacob. He sat on the floor outside his room playing with the ever-present toy horse, pushing it across the floor.

"Uncle John," the child sprang to his feet, "You are here, really here. You didn't leave!"

"Boy, what are you doing up? It is early." John whispered as he crept into the hallway, closed his own bedroom door. "Everyone is still asleep. You must go back to bed."

"But I wanted to make sure you were still here. I thought maybe I dreamed of seeing you."

"Child, now you see it is not a dream. Come, run to your room and go back to bed."

Stubborn and defiant like his uncle, Jacob stood his ground. "Uncle John, please come back to our house like you used to, and take me and Joshua on rides on your horse. You can dress up in your costumes and read from your books and, and--"

Jacob stopped mid-sentence, the reality of the situation too much for the little heart to hold. He knew the truth. Everything had changed. Tears threatened to fall.

John's heart lurched in pain. "Jacob, do you know how to dress yourself?"

"Yes," sniffled the young boy.

"Then do it quietly and we will walk together outside. I will show you the place by the swimming pond where your grandfather would sit quietly with me. Would that please you, boy?"

"Yes, Uncle John."

"Then be quick and quiet. I will meet you in the front parlor."

John went back into his room and silently found his boots and tidied his hastily thrown on clothes. He was fearful to wake Emma, her shoulder still healing, her need for rest great. He gazed upon her sleeping form, her golden silken strands of hair as soft as corn silk splayed out upon the pillows. At this moment, her sweet fair face was at peace. But as he turned to go his boots scuffed the floor. At the noise, her eyes fluttered open and she sat up, bolting upright as panic quickly blanched her face.

"What is it John? What is going on? Where are you going? You cannot leave without me."

"Emma my love, rest your mind. I am only going out for a walk with Jacob. He awoke and thought seeing me was a dream last night. He was sitting outside our door on the floor playing with his toy waiting for me. I could not convince him to go back to bed."

Emma's worried countenance relaxed as she heard her husband recount the early morning's events.

"Well, then you must go to him. He is an extraordinary boy, so devoted to you and his mother. The first time I saw him at Asia's home in Philadelphia, it was like looking at you as a little boy. Even though I was terrified that Asia would not believe me, seeing Jacob made me even more resolved to convince her that you were alive."

"For your courage, wife, I am eternally grateful."

John bent to kiss Emma. Making her comfortable again, he gently covered her again as she slipped under the quilt to get more sleep. He glanced back before closing the door, feeling as if each time he took leave of her it might be his last.

John quietly made his way downstairs to the first floor where Jacob stood waiting by the front door. His eagerness pleased him.

"Ah Jacob, my boy." He surveyed the state of his clothes, all properly attired now. "Come now, let me see." He pretended to adjust the collar of his shirt, smooth imaginary wrinkles from his pants. "Yes, you are indeed a grown-up boy now, all dressed up by yourself and ready to go. Come, let's go and walk."

With that John took his little nephew's hand and felt the silky smoothness of the young boy's skin next to his. How he loved this child. He would love his own even more. Together they made their way onto the front porch and onto the expansive front lawn. It was a beautiful morning. The dew-covered grass lay out before them like a carpet of green velvet and the scents of an early summer dawn greeted them, fragrant and intoxicating.

Edwin awoke with a start, the sound of distant voices startling him from sleep. His room overlooked the front portion of the house. Rising quickly from his bed to peer out the window, he saw John and Jacob walking across the lawn, hand in hand.

The love between the two was visible with each step. Edwin watched them walk and talk until the thicket of trees that guarded the pond cut them from his view. Regardless of his horrendous crimes or how misguided his reasoning was it was clear John had much good inside his heart.

"My God," Edwin lamented, "Whatever are we to do?"

Lacking strength, feeling torn apart inside, he dropped to his knees beside the bed, devoutly pouring out his heart in prayer.

"Dear Lord, I am forever thankful for the life you have spared. Surely, in your wisdom and mercy you have reasons for saving our Johnny, for allowing him a second chance to move forward as a husband, brother, uncle, and soon to be father. Judgement is yours, not mine. Please give me guidance as how to keep him safe. Help me protect John's wife, their unborn child and restore what is right to our family. We have lost so much."

It was then Edwin bowed his head into his hands, the tears for all his family falling shamelessly from his inky black eyes.

━━━━━ ◆ ━━━━━

In the quiet of the walk John reflected back to the day of Emma's recovery in Richmond that eventually brought them both to Tudor Hall. A beautiful spring May morning, just a short time ago? Or was it a lifetime ago? John turned to his nephew, stopped in mid-step and said to him, "You are the light in my eye and in my heart, remember that always Jacob, remember that always."

The young boy turned and lifted his handsome face, "Uncle John, I will love you always, I promise." He looked at the ground, a frown etched on his lips. "I just don't understand all that has happened."

John knelt to face the young boy, his heart bursting with admiration for his nephew, took his hands in his. "Child feel my hands, feel the life and warmth going through them."

"I feel them. Yours are big. Mine are small."

"You will choose to do good things and grow-up to be a very good, honorable man. You will not harm others, do things that cause pain."

"Did you hurt someone?" He quietly asked.

"Yes, I did. It was wrong."

"I would give anything to have it back the way it was."

John saw a wise soul inside Jacob's eyes. Someday he would hear of the assassination, know the unforgivable details.

"As would I."

They continued walking. The path through the thicket of trees led them to the glistening swimming pond. The water stood still as glass reflecting the early morning sun and promise of yet another sweltering day.

"Uncle John," exclaimed Jacob, "Is this the pond where you swam when you were a boy?"

John smiled and indulged the child, "Yes, I always loved this pond. It was right about here," he pointed to the embankment, "on this small bank of rock just above the pond's edge where your grandfather would bring me on mornings just like this. He would stroke my hair and talk to me. We would look at the water below us and the sky above and he would hold me tight as we sat up here on the edge, so I did not fall. Would you like to sit up there with me?"

Jacob nodded. Guiding him along the edge, John gestured to him to sit upon the same bank of rocks. The edge was steep, going straight down. But John settled beside him and Jacob climbed upon his uncle's lap and nestled his face against his uncle's soft cotton shirt.

"What did Grandfather talk to you about?"

John looked down at the still blue water, unbroken by even a single ripple; his mind wishing life could be so smooth and clear. "He would say, 'Tis your father's favorite you are, my son.' And he liked to say that life is like the pond. When we cast stones into the water, it sends ripples that touch every rock and reed. Some are good and beautiful and some are not. Much like our actions, the things we do affect everyone especially those we love."

"I will be good I promise Uncle John."

"And you will forever remember this day and what I have told you?"

John watched as his nephew's lips quiver as he absorbed the deeper meaning, the confession that his sins touched everyone in the Booth family. The boy was no longer a child. The past few months had changed everyone, even this innocent child. Jacob now knew that even his beloved Uncle could make mistakes.

John gathered his nephew in his arms as they watched the sun rise just over the pond. Sunlight kissed the trees, filtering through the green leaves, and glistening upon the water. Finding momentary peace inside, he began to gently comb and stroke the silky strands of his nephew's jet black curls, finding rare contentment in the stillness of the early morning.

◆

Their quiet reflection enjoyed in that early morning visit to the swimming pond was dispelled by the sound through the trees of Asia calling to her son, "Jacob! Where are you? Jacob!"

"See here, we have worried your mother. We must return to the house, we don't want to upset her."

The young boy sprang up, and turned to go. Then he stopped, looked at John with all seriousness. "I know there men who are after you. Uncle Edwin wants you to hide. I heard him talk to Mama. They called you John Singer, I don't understand why they called you that. But if you leave, where will you and Aunt Emma go?"

John smiled down at his nephew and roughened the silken locks of black curls and said gently, "Ease your mind son, and go to your mother now."

With that said Jacob ran full out toward the sound of his mother's call. John heard the young boy's voice break the peace of the quiet of the morning, "I am here Mother. I am here!"

John sat there for several moments at the edge of the pond gathering his thoughts. Today would be difficult. Today he must say goodbye, maybe forever.

When he returned to the house, he saw Asia standing on the front lawn of the house hugging Jacob. Her worry at his disappearance had brought tears. He knew he could not stay at Tudor Hall much longer. Edwin's words of how the family was in danger because of him resonated within. He must take Emma and begin their life in hiding. Or, he must convince Emma to stay in Richmond, a much safer place. Head bent in thought, his shoulders stooped as he continued his walk. The harsh reality of his hiding in plain sight and the reality of his life on the run weighed heavy upon him. It was time.

As he continued to walk towards his boyhood home, Asia and Jacob stood together on the front porch, waiting for him to join them. She tried to smile. "Our time together as a family is running short, brother. Edwin has secured a home for you. He spoke of it last night. There is a small house and farm in the Shenandoah Valley between Winchester and Martinsburg. It's one of few remaining standing after the Union swept through at the end of the war and burned most of the countryside. The name of the farm is Aurora after the Roman goddess of the dawn."

John wondered at the odd name, "Aurora?"

"Yes, the mythical Roman goddess of the dawn. Perhaps it is an omen that you and Emma and the baby will be forever protected."

"I hope that is true."

John felt grateful for the help of his family and followed Asia and Jacob into the house.

They were barely past the threshold when Edwin met them, silent yet resolved. John noticed the all too familiar expression of sorrow and grief in his brother's eyes. A pang of regret once again swept through his heart knowing that every family member present at Tudor Hall was in harm's way.

Edwin turned to Asia and said gently, "Please see to Emma's comfort and help her to pack. Quickly now. Jacob, you go and help your mother tend to your brothers."

Jacob lifted his head sullenly and murmured, "Yes, sir." But as Jacob made his way to the stairwell he turned suddenly and cried out, "Uncle John, please don't go!"

The pain of saying goodbye assailed the young boy, his cries wracking his small body. Asia went to her son and knelt to face him. She stroked his cheek and wiped his tears away.

"Child, we must do what Uncle Edwin says now. Uncle John and Aunt Emma will be safe. We will see them again. We know where they are. We just won't be able to visit them for a while."

"It isn't forever?"

"No, not forever. Only for now. Maybe at Christmas, when the new baby comes, we can visit."

The promise felt hollow, even to John's ears, but that distant hope appeased Jacob enough to calm down. Asia smiled through her own sense of loss and took her son's hand. The only sound then was the creaking of their shoes on the hardwood stairs as they ascended to the second floor.

Edwin was anxious, his feet unable to stay still as he paced back and forth, quickly laying out the plans for John and Emma's escape from society, their move to the Shenandoah.

"I know both you and Emma just arrived here to Tudor Hall, but you must be aware of the dangers. Not only to our family, but now to good Mrs. Rogers. As I mentioned last night, when Asia told me you were alive and hiding as John Singer, I already arranged for your passage to the Shenandoah. We have a wagon and have loaded it with supplies. Make haste now." Edwin's hand was upon John's back, pushing him toward the door. "It is time to leave."

John was shocked by the immediate dismissal. "But what of Mother? She is at Mrs. Rogers with Junius and Rosalie. I have to say goodbye to mother."

"Johnny," retorted Edwin, "There is no time."

John responded back fiercely, "I am not leaving without saying goodbye to mother. Why was she sent away with Mrs. Rogers last night? This is her home. She should be here with us now!"

Edwin's frustrations mounted, too much to bear as he shouted, "Mother is with Mrs. Rogers because your leaving Tudor Hall with her here could kill her."

With that said John raced out the front door and headed to the farm of their neighbor. John ran hard, his own guilt and grief pushing him forward. Childhood memories of days gone by spent at the Rogers farm assailed John; he knew today's memory would be a heartbreaking one. Yet he had to see his mother, perhaps, he thought for the last time.

He knocked gently at the front door, all the while catching his breath from his run across the forest and open fields. John waited for a moment as the door swung open and dear Mrs. Rogers was there to greet him.

She was silent as she gestured for him to come in, John eyes all the while transfixed at the sight of his mother sitting by the open hearth in a rocking chair as if she knew like she always did of when he was in distress.

Mrs. Rogers left the room as silently as she had entered it, knowing the pain that would come of this visit. She was a devoted and a true friend to Mary Ann opening her home to the family.

The misery of the moment overwhelmed John as he ran to his mother and knelt his head upon her lap. He wrapped his arms about her slight body and sobbed uncontrollably.

"I'm sorry, Mother. I'm so sorry."

While he lamented, Mrs. Booth stroked her son's hair as she had done so many times as a child, "Son, do not cry. Come; let me see your handsome face. Look at me, son."

John slowly raised his face to meet his mother's eyes, the eyes of the woman who had comforted, taught him, and loved him all his life.

"I must go."

"Yes, it is time. I cannot understand why you acted as you did; it has broken my heart beyond all that I am. They told me you were dead my son, hunted down by the Union army and killed in that barn shot through the neck. When I heard of this, I prayed that death come and beckon my door to relieve me of my grief. "But," as she offered a slight smile, "You are here. You are alive."

"Yes. No longer Booth. I must henceforth be John Singer."

"It is wise. My heart rejoiced at seeing you. But I know you must take leave of me once again, with your wife whom I can see from a mother's heart loves your dearly. And, she is with child. A child I might never see or hold. I can only hope that in leaving your family you will find safe refuge. Just know Johnny, your mother will always be your mother, and I will love you now as I did the day you were born, until the day I die."

John took his mother's hand and kissed it gently. He wanted to stay longer, but Edwin was right, danger surrounded him. He rose from his knees then and silently walked away from her, the agony of the moment too great to bear.

He heard her say under her breath, "My bright boy Absalom," before her sobbing was the last thing he heard as once again he ran through the forest, across the fields.

John had tears streaming down his face, knowing he would always be running away from family and those he loved. It was the only way to protect them. He slowed his gait long enough to wipe away the shame, steady himself.

Now he must gather Emma, say goodbye to his family and his boyhood home.

The house was eerily quiet as he entered the front door and headed up the stairs. It was if the house itself felt the terrible sadness that had once again befallen the Booth family, and it too was laden with grief. He entered the bedroom to find Emma was busily packing to leave. John silently took the shirts she was packing out of her hands and moved to wrap her in his embrace.

He whispered to his beloved, "Darlin' this is not the life I would have wanted for you. You deserve so much better than life on the run with me."

Emma held him tight.

"And now we bring a child into this mess. A baby is a blessing that I do not deserve, yet God in His mercy has given." He drew back to look at her, saying words that cut through his soul. But saying it was right. "I have endangered my family by being here. I must make things right. You would be safer with your mother in Richmond; there you will be comforted by your childhood home and familiar surroundings. You would have your mother with you when the time comes. I cannot give you anything Emma except a life on the run, fearful at every turn, hiding and denying it all."

Emma slowly stepped back from her husband's embrace. She looked him squarely in his eyes. She shook her head in defiance, "John, I will not go back to Richmond. We will go the Shenandoah together. I will never leave you, ever."

"But you must think of our baby." John moved his hands to encircle her stomach where the promise of a new life was just beginning.

"Our child needs a father. So, no more talk of living apart. I am your wife. For better or for worse. You are not John Wilkes Booth anymore. Your name is Singer. And my name is Mrs. John Singer. Understood?"

John smiled slightly, "Yes my darling, indeed you are the courageous, Mrs. John Singer."

Emma nodded upon hearing those words and then in a determined tone said to her husband, "See, I am almost finished packing. Asia is in the kitchen packing the foodstuffs that will travel well. The horse and buckboard will be ready soon as we do not know what conditions we will find at Aurora."

"Ah, so you heard the name of our new home. What do you think of it? Asia thought it would protect us, like in Roman mythology with Aurora being the goddess of dawn."

Emma simply shrugged, "Perhaps it will protect us, but let us not think too hard upon it for the mythology of the Roman Gods could just as easily be interpreted as a great tragedy, as well. For we know of the tragedy of Rome, their empire and their Gods.”

John silently agreed that indeed, tragedy could be awaiting them at every turn.

Their bags packed, John walked down the stairway from the second to the first floor, mindful of the feel of the hardwood under his boots. Outside, an old buckboard with a sturdy black horse was waiting for his passengers. He hoped the simple buckboard would bring no notice or scrutiny to them as they passed through the countryside. Mindful as so much of the Shenandoah Valley was made inhabitable in the early spring of 1865 as the Union forces swept through.

John stopped for a moment to touch the animal who would take them to safety, noticing the strip of white that crossed between his eyes. It brought back a wave of nostalgia. He was reminded then of his Cola and the days spent riding his beloved colt through the Maryland countryside.

Asia came out the front door holding a basket of dry foodstuffs for their journey. The back of the buckboard held household goods, supplies they would need. The load was covered with a cloth, secured for the long ride. No words passed as Emma was lifted on the front seat and the basket placed next to her.

Asia waited. The depth of her grief was unmistakable in her eyes.

“Even the horse given to take us on our journey will forever remind me of the days spent here with you, sister mine. Dashing through the woods on Cola, reciting Shakespeare, playing the flute. Days that are gone forever. Yet the carefree wildness of that time remains in my heart and my mind’s eye, like it was yesterday. If only I could go back, change everything.”

“Yes Johnny, those days are gone forever. But you are alive, and alive you will stay. You cannot change what you did.”

John’s head was bowed down before his sister’s words; it was too painful to face her and say goodbye, while not knowing if he would ever see her again.

“Johnny,” Asia suddenly asked “Do you have the medal?” He reached into the collar of his open shirt and produced the Agnus Dei.

Asia lightly touched it. “When you need me, hold onto it and call my name. I will come and help you. I will hear you in my dreams, just like I did before.”

“Oh Asia how dear, sweet and brave you are.”

“Remember what I told you Johnny. I will come. Always Johnny, always.”

John looked at the house, the empty front door. “Where is Jacob? I must say goodbye to him.”

Asia shook her head. "Edwin took the boys over to Mrs. Rogers to pick blackberries. He is strong, but young. It would be too hard for him to see you leave."

John swallowed hard, knowing his sister was right. He climbed into the wagon, "Goodbye sister mine, try to be happy."

John shook the reins and clicked his tongue at the horse to move forward. He did not look back to see his sister crumble to her knees in tears remembering the last time he said those words to her, but the memory assailed him, nonetheless.

It was at Asia's house in Philadelphia when she pleaded with him not to go south, his sympathy steadfast for the Confederacy. It was now a moment frozen in time. He had laid his head upon her lap and she stroked his hair and for a fleeting time a sense of peace had filled his heart.

That day, as he rose to say his goodbye to Asia, he had kissed her cheek and said, "Goodbye sister mine, try to be happy."

Only after Tudor Hall faded in the distance and his tattered emotions were once again under control did he turned his eyes toward his beloved Emma, who was silent and pale as they rode toward an uncertain future.

"Penny for your thoughts, Emma darlin?" he sweetly asked his wife.

"Oh John, I am so jumbled in my mind right now, I am not sure what I am thinking."

"It has been a long few months Emma. I feel like we have lived a lifetime in that short span of time. I can only hope and pray our journey to our new home is the start of our life together, with our darlin' Juliet to have and to hold."

"There you go again, John," as a smile parted her lips, "How is it you so sure this child is a girl?"

"Because I just know. She will be the best parts of ourselves, I know that too."

They sat quietly together then, as the buckboard lurched forward to their uncertain future. It was then his thoughts raced back several weeks to that near fatal day in June when they were staying in Richmond at Emma's family home. That day a month ago, he nearly lost her. When she awoke from her accident that had in fact been an attempt on his own life, John knew in his heart their world was forever changed. He let his thoughts wander back to the events in Richmond that now drove them forever into hiding.

CHAPTER FOUR

The Dixon Residence in Richmond, Virginia

"You'se can't be dead, you'se just can't be dead!"
~~ Old Sam

June, 1865

While riding at a full gallop from Alexandria, past the war ravaged neighborhoods of Richmond, as they came near the Dixon home, the head physician Jonas Hendrix and Old Sam heard two shots blast the air. Knowing Doctor Henry Bradley had followed Emma and John intent on proving his love to the beautiful young nurse who captured his heart, they pushed their horses faster. An unrequited love and a mystery as to who John Singer really was caused Henry's mind to darken, his thoughts and actions manic.

Doctor Hendrix and Old Sam had come to stop him. As they galloped closer Old Sam witnessed John Singer running toward the Dixon home with Miss Emma in his arms.

"No! We're too late!" shouted the good Doctor, sliding from the saddle before the horse even stopped, his medical bag already in hand. Sam joined him, not even taking time to tie up the winded horses.

Blood flowed down Emma's wounded shoulder and over her chest. Her skin looked deadly pale and her long blonde hair had fallen loose, trailing over John Singer's arm like molten gold.

The Doctor placed two fingers along her smooth throat. Sam dared not breathe.

"She's alive."

Without another word, they followed John into the house.

Inside, while the Doctor worked to save Emma, it was decided Old Sam should take Mrs. Dixon downstairs to calm and soothe the frantic mother.

But, she could not be consoled. Even when Doctor Hendrix came downstairs, announcing Emma would live, her mother was frantic at the scene that had unfolded in her very home.

Old Sam realized he did not know what had happened to Henry. "I needs to go," he announced to anyone listening, "I got to see about Henry." While Mrs. Dixon anguished over her daughter, he ran out the door. He heard it slam behind him and kept running, his big body moving faster than it had in years.

There on the barn floor lay a man whose broken mind had torn a hole in Sam's heart. He let out a wail, gathering Henry into his great arms, cradling his limp form like a bloody broken child. In his grief, he rocked back and forth, the body limp and lifeless.

Tending to patients with Doctor Bradley had been his hospital duties, one he had shouldered with care and pride. Serving Henry was the only place where Sam felt needed, felt loved.

He cried out, "You'se can't be dead, you'se just can't be. God, please don't take this one. Please, he is all I have. He didn't mean noffin' to happen to Miss Emma."

Sam sat on the barn floor holding his friend, sorrow causing deep anguished sobs to echo from the rafters, his cries reaching far beyond the room. John and Doctor Hendrix had taken Emma inside, leaving Old Sam with a man whose fragmented mind had driven him to an act of unspeakable murderous intent.

"He's sorry! I just knows it."

With that said, as if the heaven heard his cries, Henry lurched his head and moaned.

"Glory be," cried Old Sam, "Glory be, he's still alive!"

Old Sam then gently laid him in the bloodied hay and cried out to Doctor Hendrix, "He's alive, please Doc please come, come quickly and make him better. Fix him!"

"Henry, you'se gonna be jest fine, I knows it."

Henry groaned, flopped one hand as if to rub his head, but made another pained sound; his hand dropped. His eyes remained closed.

The anguished cries from the barn had reached the upstairs room where Doctor Hendrix was tending Emma. The screams that echoed through the house reminded the Doctor of the death screams from the wounded and dying soldiers that he had heard over the course of the four long years of the bloody Civil War. When he had finished with Emma, he quickly found his way to the barn to where Old Sam was cradling Henry.

"He's alive, Doc."

"Let me see." But he automatically knelt, searching for a heartbeat. Working with lightning speed he observed the oozing wound on the side of Henry's temple. The bullet had nicked the side of his face, going upward along the scalp rather than straight through. It appears in the last second, Henry's shooting hand had dropped, tipping the gun at an angle. The wound continued to bleed profusely. It was not fatal.

"Quickly now Old Sam, we must stop the bleeding." The limited supplies in his physician's bag had already been used to save Emma. "I need a compress, we must hurry."

Old Sam didn't hesitate; he tore off the well-worn shirt from his own body and gave it to the good Doctor. Without stopping for a moment, Jonas applied pressure on the wound with the rag and kept it there. They watched in dismay as the shirt was stained crimson in just a few minutes.

"We must work quickly. We need another compress, and bandages. Run into the house now, Sam. And tell Mrs. Dixon to heat some water."

Doctor Hendrix looked up at Old Sam blinking back the tears as the great hulking man ran shirtless to the Dixon house.

Old Sam bounded into the front foyer of the great house, racing to find Mrs. Dixon and do what Doctor Hendrix asked. He found her in the great parlor, weeping. She was seated with a little blond girl who looked like Emma and the Dixon's were surrounded by two black house servants. His intrusion startled them.

He stammered, aware of his shirtless hulking form and begged the mistress of the house, "Please Mrs. Dixon, forgive me, but Doc Hendrix done asked me to come and get another compress. Henry is done hurt bad, and Doc asked to please put on some water and heat it."

Mrs. Dixon felt bewildered and dazed from seeing her Emma wounded and bloodied, her son-in-law John racing her up to their bedroom, and hearing it was Henry Bradley who shot her and wounded himself. It was all too much for her heart to bear.

"Esmeralda," directed Mrs. Dixon, "Heat the water and provide Old Sam here with whatever Doctor Hendrix asks. Hurry now please."

"Charles," she instructed, "Help her."

With that, the two house servants dispersed to do the mistress's bidding. It was then Mrs. Dixon stood to meet Old Sam, demanding an explanation. "What is going on here? Please, I cannot get an answer from anyone, not Doctor Hendrix nor John. But you were at the hospital where all this trouble apparently began. You must know something. Now, tell me."

Old Sam bend his head low, he whispered to Mrs. Dixon, "I, I really don't know, 'cept that Doc Bradley was powerful upset about Miss Emma marrying Mr. John."

"He was jealous?"

"He, he was just so upset, is all." Sam hated to lie, but refused to say anything that might cause Henry more trouble. "He didn't mean to hurt Miss Emma. I can't say noffin' more, Ma'am. I best be getting back to help Doc Hendrix."

With that said, Old Sam charged out of the Dixon home and back into the stables to help Doctor Hendrix where the two house servants had already brought needed supplies.

He said as much as he could, not willing to share the remainder of what drove Henry to this maddening act. The truth was much too deep for casually sharing with Emma's mother and that was Henry's conviction that John Singer was an imposter and was really John Wilkes Booth.

Once Henry's wound had been dressed, the bleeding stopped and the gash across his temple stitched, they had to decide what to do with him. He could not stay in the stables. Knowing there would be much anger and animosity toward the man who tried to kill John but shot Emma instead, Doctor Hendrix sent one of the house servants to ask permission to bring him inside the house.

Mrs. Dixon was reluctant, but sent word she would allow Henry into her home. He was settled temporarily into the little bedroom in the back corner of the Dixon home, tucked away near the kitchen. He had awakened briefly when Doctor Hendrix and Old Sam moved him, thrashed around, cried out and then drifted into unconsciousness again.

Doctor Hendrix went to find Mrs. Dixon, realizing so much horror had transpired to her family in so short a time. He felt the need to sit with her and try to console her as much as he could. He remembered how gracious she appeared, even in such horrific circumstances. He only saw her at a glance during the emergency with Emma, but noticed how lovely she had looked, even in such distress and realized where Emma had found her beauty.

He found her in the front parlor, a young blonde girl sitting next to her, sharing words of comfort that seemingly were doing no good. The mistress of the house looked up as Jonas stood motionless in the parlor, not willing to intrude further in her obvious private moments with her younger daughter.

As she composed herself from the intense discussion with her daughter, Mrs. Dixon rose to greet the man that had saved her daughter's life. She walked towards him in a way that was regal yet approachable and as she extended her hand in greeting, said in a lovely drawl, "My home is yours, sir. I can offer you all that have and would offer you more if I had it, for I know there is nothing more precious than life. And for saving the life of Emma, what I have is at your disposal. You are welcome to stay, for as long as you wish. I am most sincerely in debt to your skill as a physician and to your kindness."

It had been a very long time since he had been in the presence of a true lady. With the war bringing such chaos and destruction, it seems so many genteel customs and social manners had been discarded. Pleased she saw fit to behave with dignity on such an upsetting day, Doctor Hendrix took her hand and raised it to his lips and then politely released it.

"Mrs. Dixon, it is I who am humbled and grateful for the gift of sparing young lives. My hands are but instruments of God, and I can only save those He allows me to save."

With a gentle wave of her hand she beckoned the Doctor to sit next to her on the settee. "Please, come rest for a moment. You rode all the way from Alexandria. You must be exhausted."

He followed her and sat down. "This is my daughter, Abby." She introduced the pre-teen girl, who nodded and smiled. "I have asked our Esmeralda to bake some biscuits with gravy. I realize it not the grand a meal I would normally want to serve, but you are welcome to take your fill."

He felt grateful for her hospitality.

"Abby," she motioned to her young daughter, "I know you want to learn to bake. Can you please help Esmerelda in the kitchen? I believe there may be some sugar and flour left, perhaps enough for a sweet cake."

"Oh yes, Mother. I love when Esmerelda teaches me to cook." Abby hugged her mother then and gently curtseyed to the Doctor before finding her way to the kitchen.

It was only then Doctor Hendrix spoke, "Mrs. Dixon, right now biscuits and gravy sounds wonderful. I did not realize how hungry I am. So much has happened; I have not eaten at all today. I am very thankful for the simple meal."

Mrs. Dixon inhaled a deep breath, "I realize a great calamity has befallen us all today with my Emma being shot, and by the hand of our friend, Henry Bradley. Why would he do that? Young Henry was a part of this household his whole life. He and his family were guests at numerous occasions. Emma even left us after her father and brother died in First Manassas to work as a nurse in Alexandria, knowing Henry was a surgeon there."

He nodded, knowing this. "She is a strong, courageous woman. We needed her skills, greatly."

"Then I ask you now Doctor Hendrix, what happened at that hospital? Did something occur to trigger this madness in Henry, for what else could it be, for the change that has so obviously taken place?"

Doctor Hendrix thought for a moment, mulling over the words that he knew would sound irrational and shocking to the mistress, yet as he paused his eyes lingered a bit too long for proper decorum over the appealing countenance of Mrs. Dixon.

It had been a very long time since he even thought about another woman. His wife, Mary, had been gone now these last four years, a victim too of the war. At her insistence, she came to the hospital early in the war to stay together and to help her husband, but instead she caught typhoid fever, dying a painful death. The loss had left him numb to the sight of another woman.

Except for now. "Mrs. Dixon," he began, "I will tell you all I know and beg your forgiveness at the outrageousness of what I will say, for most certainly it is quite unbelievable, but please, I ask before I begin, what is your first name?”

Instead of chiding her guest for his familiarity, she smiled. “Of course. I would be very please for you to call me Annabelle.”

Doctor Hendrix signed and shook his head, a slight smile curled his lips as he confessed to his lovely hostess, “I beg your pardon, but I must state this truth, Annabelle is a most favored name of mine.”

“How is it Annabelle came to be your favorite name?”

He bowed his head in deference to her, somewhat embarrassed for having admitted the favoritism, “From a poem. It’s the name of my favorite work by Edgar Allen Poe, entitled Annabel Lee.”

“Ah yes I am familiar with the poem. It is a lament by Mr. Poe about love and the loss of his dear young wife.” She tipped her head, considering a deeper meaning, “It’s perhaps no strange circumstance then that I share that name, as well, for the love and loss that has befallen me.”

“I believe the war had inflicted much loss, to all.”

She then nodded, lowered her eyes to consider those thoughts, “And your first name, Doctor Hendrix?”

“It’s Jonas.”

Annabelle smiled, soft and lovely. “Please then, Jonas, help me understand today’s event. I believe something happened to Henry at the hospital. Poor Emma has only recently come home with her John, whom she deeply loves. And he adores her. I am happy for Emma to have found happiness. We just barely finished her wedding and her life as a wife is just beginning. To think I almost lost her, felled by a bullet from one of our oldest and dearest neighbors. Please, I beg you as parent, regardless of how you think the tale may sound, tell me.”

Jonas swallowed hard at her request of him, it was all so incredulous, yet he knew he would tell her the truth. “As the chief surgeon and administrator of the Alexandria Field Hospital, my duties were to the wounded soldiers who passed through our doors, as well as insuring the health and safety of our physicians, nurses and caregivers.”

“For four years I watched and worked to save lives as so many of our dear comrades left this world in the most horrifying conditions. Unfortunately for many soldiers, they died before I ever had the chance to help them. Often the influx of wounded overwhelmed us. I carry this agony within my heart, hearing the begging of the soldiers around me, and I unable to tend them.”

“Such was the magnitudes of death and destruction,” Annabelle commiserated his experiences.

Jonas nodded, continuing, “In the days after the end of the war, we were all beyond exhausted, none more so than Henry. Not only is he a talented surgeon, but he carried his compassion to the extreme."

"What do you mean?"

"Henry felt the loss of so many personally, almost like it was his fault they died. For instance, I was nearby when Henry was saying farewell to a North Carolina soldier who was being released as ambulatory. The man was ever so grateful for his life, yet Henry remained grievous that he could not save his arm. To me, it went beyond professional compassion, but the concern exhibited by Henry is a hallmark of deep and abiding humanity."

"To be sure, his compassion it is quite evident."

Jonas was quick to agree, "Yes too much so, it seems."

"How so?"

"What I will tell you now was recounted to me by a visiting nurse. She and Henry became very good friends. Her name was Louisa May Alcott. She had come to serve in the early days of the war, but had to leave due to typhoid fever. Yet, her heart remained. It brought her back around, from time to time. She felt indebted to our Henry for the care and concern he gave her over the loss of one particular soldier, a man she found favor with, and who later passed away."

"That's terrible, to find love and have it stolen away."

"Yes, stolen, indeed. Something I believe Henry also felt." Annabelle gave him a curious questioning look. "You see, recently I was visited upon by Miss Alcott, who had returned to Alexandria in the last days of the war. Being a kind compassionate woman, she carefully described to me a conversation she had with Henry that disturbed her. So much so, it brought her to my door in the deepest distress, consumed by worry. It seems that Henry had confided in Louisa of unrequited feelings of Miss Emma."

"Oh my! I knew he cared for her but well the war came and Emma went to work at the hospital in Alexandria because Henry was there and felt a friendship towards him. I never realized the depth of his feelings."

"Quite the opposite, I'm afraid. These feelings were exacerbated and deeply troubling to Henry with a rival for his affections. It seems the last ambulance coming to our hospital in early May, brought with it a certain soldier named John Singer."

Annabelle sat up a little straighter, her eyes brighter as she was keenly interested in hearing the details of how Emma had met John. "Do tell, Jonas. Please continue."

"I can only recount my understanding. Miss Emma found much favor with the man, It was obvious to all who saw them, they held deep feelings for one another. I understand he had been found on a dirt road unconscious, suffering from a broken leg. It had a makeshift cast on it, but the bones were not set properly, causing him great pain. He was fortunate the leg would heal and no gangrene was present to his wounds. But soon he was affected by malaria. His fever was raging. Henry was his attending physician and believed the man to be quite beyond any medical help."

"Yet, somehow he lived."

"Emma risked her life by entering the secluded ward and tended him, begging Henry to dispel the last of our quinine to help him. It worked. She saved him. From that time Emma and John were wholly devoted to one another, happy to have love in the midst of such pain and suffering."

"It should have been a happy ending," Annabelle surmised, "Yet we know from today, their happiness caused Henry much pain."

"Indeed, it did. Perhaps it was exhaustion that addled Henry's mind, but his objection to Emma loving this man was frightening. He openly ranted she was his. He claimed he had waited until after the war to have his feelings for her be known. Not knowing the depth of his secret affections, Emma in her honesty and open heart, had confided to Henry of her feelings to John. For her, she was simply speaking to him as a neighbor, a physician and a friend. She claimed her heart belonged to John and only John."

"I can imagine the impact this had on poor Henry."

"It pushed him over the edge." Jonas shook his head as he recalled the events. "Henry's rantings became worse. You see, Old Sam is his truest companion and friend. He is eternally loyal to Henry and confided that Miss Emma had found John's diary in the pile of uniforms ready to be burnt."

"A diary? She was sure it was John's?"

"Positive. According to Old Sam, who saw it too, it contained many news clippings, a letter and a copy of the WANTED poster for the capture of John Wilkes Booth."

Annabelle gasped, clutched at her heart. "The assassin who shot our President Lincoln?"

"Yes. Since his appearance well is rather similar, Old Sam thought perhaps John Singer and John Wilkes Booth to be one and the same. But Emma did not care, her love being all that mattered. She asked Old Sam to say nothing of finding the diary. You have met him. Old Sam is a simple obedient man. In his friendship to Miss Emma, he had acquiesced."

"Why would Old Sam tell Henry?"

"Purely out of worry for his friend. As the eventualities of John and Emma's relationship were known throughout the hospital, it seemed to agitate Henry further and further into despair. He chose to firmly believe the rumor. A gentleman who regularly visited the hospital, Walt Whitman, the great author and poet, was also Henry's friend. Upon one visit, Mr. Whitman casually mentioned he thought

John Singer bore a strong resemblance to John Wilkes Booth and, as his questions directly to John about the most basic of information went unanswered, he brought his misgivings to Henry."

"Oh no Jonas, no!"

"Henry blamed John Singer for his misery, for stealing Emma and yes, he believed he was indeed Booth. Rumors grew into outright arguments. Emma staunchly denied it. Yet, Henry raged. It was then Miss Alcott brought the situation to my attention. She begged me to talk to Henry and help in whatever way I could. After speaking with him, seeing with my own eyes his exhaustion and ranting, I took him off medical rotation for a few days and sent Old Sam to stay with him, with orders to rest and eat. But he is a stubborn, single-minded man."

"He did not rest?"

"Not at all. Especially after Emma left, coming here with John. The ideas festered in his mind. His unrequited love turned to a vengeful anger, a fury raging inside that burned away all right or reason. I was horrified to see it. I instructed Old Sam to keep Henry locked inside. But he escaped, eluding his friend and sentry. If it weren't for the stable boy Isaac who pounded on my door, relaying to me that Henry had taken my horse to find John and Emma here in Richmond, I would not have known to come here. Old Sam was beside himself with worry. Isaac said Henry's eyes were that of a madman. He went speeding off into the night, saying he would kill John."

Considering the tale, her chin lifted, "Jonas, thank you for telling me what you knew. Indeed, Henry is quite delusional as these were the actions of an addled mind. For regardless of how much our John resembles Mr. Booth, everyone knows the assassin was killed on April 26, just a few months ago."

Jonas nodded, listening to her conclusions. He could see Annabelle was upset by the accusations.

"His death is a known fact." She fumed, a frown marring her pretty features, "Also, what is so compelling about a diary that contained WANTED posters of Booth? I'm sure many men had one. Perhaps our John wanted it as a remembrance of the President. I can assure you that my son-in-law is a gentleman of the highest order. He will prove to be a loving husband and family member.

"Of this, I do not doubt," Jonas softly soothed, "Dear sweet Emma could not love a man who was not a gentleman."

"War changes us, forces us to do things to survive we never thought possible, yet we do them. I believe I can forgive Henry, knowing now the misery he has endured for so long. To have kept his feeling silent for so many years, as well as the pain of unrequited love and the loss of Emma to a rival certainly took its toll on his mind."

He felt relieved she had quickly come to that conclusion.

"Jonas," she had reached a decision, "His family is just a few miles from here. Henry is resting in the back room, much too injured to travel. But we must send word. His family needs to know of these horrible events."

"I agree."

"As soon as he is well enough," she stood and smoothed the skirts of her blue dress, signaling their discussion was concluded. "I want him removed from my home."

"Old Sam and I will arrange it." He stood too, suddenly feeling immensely grateful for meeting Annabelle, regardless of the circumstances. He almost wished they could sit and talk about more civilized things.

"Thank you." Her pale complexion grew warmer with relief. "We must keep him away from John and Emma. Please arrange for his care. I do not wish to cause him more injury than what he already inflicted on himself, but it is best he leave as soon as possible. I have already lost my only son and my husband to the cause. The war is over, and I will do everything in my power to have no more of my family buried."

With that said Annabelle raised her hand to Jonas, whereupon he took the smooth fingers, and lightly kissed the back of it. Her skin was warm, her touch so gentle as if touched by the wings of an angel.

He smiled and bowed with respect to his hostess as he prepared to take his leave.

"Annabelle if I may be so bold, after I have set Henry to his care, I will need to go back to the field hospital in Alexandria to arrange some things there, I am planning to return to Richmond soon after that, may I perhaps pay a call to you upon my return?"

Jonas waited what seemed an eternity as Annabelle smiled so sweet, proving she had enjoyed their interlude, too. "Why Jonas, I would be sorely disappointed if you did not."

The stillness of the Dixon house that night was a welcome respite from the day's horrifying events. Emma lay asleep, her breathing regular and soft. John maintained his vigil by her side, his eyes focused on her sleeping form. Doctor Hendrix and Old Sam were resting in one of the many upstairs bedrooms of the Dixon's house. Their beddings had been hastily constructed of whatever linens that could be found and used for their comfort.

Mrs. Dixon's fine embroidered tablecloth that was once the centerpiece of her famous dinner parties, now covering the sleeping form of Old Sam.

The restlessness from worry and stress roused John from his vigil at Emma's bedside. He paced the bedroom floor. His thoughts were racing; the quiet of the house seemed deafening, only adding to his restlessness.

He heard Henry was not only still alive, but was in this house in the back bedroom, the very room in which John had laid in the hours before his wedding.

Alive. The utter cruel irony.

John rubbed his temples with both hands as if trying to wipe away all that he had wrought in these past two months. Try as he did to wipe away the past, when he opened his eyes nothing had changed and the burden and pain in his heart only seem to intensify.

And he knew why.

He had to see Henry with his own eyes.

He quietly crept out from the room he shared with Emma, his footsteps making no sound on the torn carpet runner as he walked the long hallway toward the grand staircase. He crept along the side of the stairs as he lightly touched each marble step as he descended to the foyer. His hand reached for the wall sliding down past the imprints of the frames of the lost artwork, artwork that had once graced the grand staircase.

So much had been lost to the war. The soldiers had ravaged the Dixon home. Yet, they were also fortunate it was not burned, that their home was still standing.

John made his way to the kitchen and the small alcove to see for himself where Henry lay, alive. He entered the small bedroom, the tiny mirror above the well-worn dresser reflecting his shadowy figure as he passed by. A single oil lamp had been left burning at the bedside table, casting faint light, the wick turned low. Left there by Doctor Hendrix, perhaps, to enable him to check on his patient during the night.

He knelt beside the slim, slight form of Henry, his breathing regular now too, and noticed the dressing for his head wound was slightly stained red. It must still be bleeding.

"You should have died in that barn, Henry." John quietly rasped the angry words, "So now we both share the weight of having escaped not only sure death, but we both know the feeling of a bullet piercing the skin by our own hands. Although it appears yours did not properly do its job. Even in suicide, you have failed."

Henry did not stir his skin ghostly pale and he lay utterly still except for the rise and fall of his chest.

"I could kill you now and snuff out your life, and who would know, dying from the wound on your head? The very wound you caused to yourself, attempting to end your own life."

John shook his head, knowing he would not cause further harm. "For what you have wrought and caused not me but Emma, death should be your just deserves!"

Again, the sincere wish for Henry's death haunted John's mind, but his conscience won out. The man's fate was in the hands of God, not his own.

"I am already stained with another's blood," he hissed in frustration, "I will not add yours. As much I so deeply desire for you to leave this life, perhaps living is a worst punishment. Indeed, you will suffer. The woman you covet will never be yours. She is mine. The child she carries is mine. Her life is bound with mine."

"And so I say to you, maybe I am Booth, maybe I am not. You will never really know. And you will never have proof. So be it. May your mad lamenting be the poison that indeed will kill you."

John stood up then and prepared to leave the room. As his back was turned to leave, it was then the Henry's eyes opened and he stared at the familiar shadowy figure leave the close confines of the room.

In his hazy delirium, he cried out, "Booth!"

John stood at the threshold of the door, smiled slightly and nodded and left. Henry closed his eyes. Perhaps the pain was playing havoc with his mind. But no, he looked at the doorway again, feeling certain a moment ago a man had been there.

"He lives, he still lives." He muttered to the empty room, "And what of Emma? Oh, dear Lord. I remember," he reached up, held his aching head, "I killed her. I am sure of it."

The thought broke his already ravaged heart.

Within the space of a breath, his sorrow turned to rage. "For this Booth, no matter where you go or try to hide, I will find you. I will hunt you down like the murderer you are and kill you."

He stared at the ceiling, the darkened room seeming to fill with even more shadows. It didn't matter, nor did he understand that his own intentions to commit murder were equally heinous; exactly like the crime against humanity he was furious at John Wilkes Booth for committing.

But to Henry, his was justified. "Revenge for my Emma and for President Lincoln, I vow this with the last drop of blood I have left in me." His aching head made it hard to think. "The diary, the diary, there is proof in that diary; I must find it before it is destroyed!" That was his last thought as the pain from his wound ripped through his head blinding him from any further thoughts.

CHAPTER FIVE

The Dixon Residence in Richmond, Virginia

"I will contact Asia."
~~ John Wilkes Booth

The late afternoon June sun shone its waning rays onto the bed where the young woman rested. For two days she had hovered between unconsciousness and moments of awareness.

She had woken with clarity long enough to tell John they were expecting a child.

It was news he was stunned to hear. John had not left her side except when her mother sat in his stead, and forced him to rest. His heart was in pieces, his thoughts dark with regret.

His wife. His love. His child.

She had almost died.

Sitting beside her bed in a chair, alone in the bedroom where she lay hovering between death and life, he wept.

In her sleep, Emma drew a deeper breath. The sound made him blink, swipe away tears from his eyes.

John reached out, held her hand.

With that touch her ice blue eyes had fluttered with life. Then Emma had looked into the joyful face of her husband. As she shifted in the bed to move closer to him, the pain from her shoulder wound rifled through her slim frame causing her beautiful face to wince in agony. It was then he leaned closer, his face near hers.

"Emma. You are awake. You have come back to me!"

"What happened?"

"You were shot."

"I don't remember," her soft voice was weak.

"Oh Emma," he whispered, "I am so sorry, my darling. Oh, such a horrifying situation has befallen us. It grieves me to share this with you. I am deeply disturbed to think that madman, Doctor Bradley followed us here for the very reason to hunt me down and kill me. He believed once I was out of the way, you would see he was the better man and marry him."

"Henry was here?" She questioned, struggling to remember. "Yes, I knew he believed I might love him. But, he was wrong."

"Oh Emma," he lamented, remembering, "When he raised his pistol intending to kill me, I thought for sure the angel of death had finally come."

"No, not you," she whispered.

"But in a moment that flashed with gunpowder, you stepped in front of me. The bullet hit your shoulder. Seeing the bullet strike you and not I, his intended target, Henry must have thought that he killed you. I admit, when it first happened, I thought it might have been true. There was so much blood."

Just retelling the details was enough to make John's heart lurch, a pain tightening his core.

"While I held you in the barn, I heard the gun cock, then another gunshot. I looked up in time to see Henry's body fall, the side of his head bleeding. He shot himself in the temple. If not for Old Sam and Doctor Hendrix arriving, you might have died."

Emma held his hand while he recounted the events, trying to understand what had happened. She asked him, "Why did they suddenly appear?"

"They rode in great haste from Alexandria to stop Henry. They knew he was not right, in his mind. The stable boy Isaac had told Doctor Hendrix what happened in the barn the night Henry took his horse and the frightening look in his eyes."

She lay still for several moments, thinking.

"I remember now," she finally decided. Her brow was still creased with worry, "I saw the gun pointed at you and Henry unsteady on his feet. Then I remember feeling this horrible irrational fear that you were going to die, but it all goes dark."

"Oh Emma," John shook his head, "After the bullet struck you, I lost all sense of time. I picked you up and raced to the house. I saw Doctor Hendrix and Old Sam riding furiously up the road. They saw you hurt in my arms and followed me inside. Your poor mother screamed, seeing you bloodied and unconscious."

"My mother, oh my."

"Yes, she was beside herself, horrified. But I ran upstairs and laid you down here, in the bed. It was Old Sam who assured your mother that Doctor Hendrix was a fine physician and took her out of the room so you could be examined. I stayed right here Emma, for your procedure and assisted him."

She gave his hand a light squeeze.

"After he bandaged you up and turned to leave, we heard a man screaming from the stable, sounds like knife wounds driving right into one's very soul."

"Old Sam had found Henry?"

He nodded. "Emma, it was like nothing I had ever heard before, the sound of those screams so excruciating to one's heart, it was more primal than human. Doctor Hendrix ran out to the barn. By some miracle or fate, it seems the bullet had only grazed the side of Henry's head. He was badly hurt and bleeding profusely but did not die. But his mind is addled."

"Where is he?"

"Downstairs, in the small bedroom off the kitchen. His family will be notified of this terrible event."

Growing weary, needing to sleep, Emma sighed and closed her eyes. "It seems the casualties of this war," she whispered nearly to herself, "Are not just for the ones who have died on the battlefield."

She slept again for many hours.

John never left her side.

It was deep into the night when at last she stirred. Although it was after midnight, he made her eat, gave her soup and tea. It seemed to give her strength. A fresh light of hope came to her green eyes.

"You should eat too, my love."

"I have. I only care for you, right now. Oh Emma, the past months have been just too much to bear, and now with your injury, and to think I caused it! Forgive me, please."

John carefully reached for Emma's hand, longing to feel her embrace, knowing he deserved none of her love. To his surprise, he saw a slight smile across her sweet lips.

"My dearest husband," she softly replied, "In all this tragedy, the pain and suffering, there is a great joy I just remembered that we will someday share." Her smile widened. "Something beautiful, innocent, and pure."

Her brow creased. "Perhaps I dreamed it, but I feel sure I told you about it," as her hand slid down to her belly.

John smiled too.

"Yes, darling. You did wake for a while that very first day. We have not spoken of it again. Are you certain you are pregnant?"

She nodded. "I had to wait to be sure. I'm seven or eight weeks. The baby will come in December."

"Our child Emma our child."

"Regardless of so much horror around us, God has blessed us. Don't you see the miracle? So much death around us at the hospital, yet we found love. Now against all that has gone wrong, God blesses us with a new life to love and cherish."

John's heart lightened, "As I sat here, waiting for you to heal and wake, I thought about our child."

"Oh, John can you honestly believe this?"

He gave Emma a smile and said, "When do you think it happened?"

"I am most certain it happened the first time we were intimate together, under the pink petals of the dogwood trees. In one golden afternoon, my life was forever changed. When I looked into your eyes and knew I would love you forever."

John leaned closer to kiss her gently, but for him that softness still ignited a fire. As always with her an overwhelming desire swept over him. With Emma, it would always feel as if he were a thirsty man, satisfied momentarily with the sweetness of her, then left thirsty again. He pulled away reluctantly, mindful of her shoulder injury and the precious child within her.

His child.

A second chance, not just to love her, but a second chance in life, one he knew he did not deserve.

Hope welled within him.

Her eyes were blinking slower again. Sleep hovered. But her skin was no longer sickly pale. A slight flush now colored her cheeks, the hand in his felt warmer.

He tucked the blankets around her, settling into his nightly vigil by her side. "Darlin' Emma, it's time for you to rest now. There will be more time to show our love. But tonight, you must rest and heal."

◆

John woke at dawn as someone was shaking his shoulder, telling him to wake up. He opened his eyes to realize exhaustion had overtaken him and he had fallen asleep with his head upon Emma's stomach, his arms wrapped around her body in a possessive and protective hug.

"Wake up, John. I must speak with you."

The urgency in her voice had him sitting upright. The reason for the shooting skated across his tired mind, fear replaced comfort as he instantly was at high alert. He stood, looked about the bedroom, seeing only the familiar furnishings.

"What has happened?"

She sat up away from the pillows, heedless of her pain. "Dearest John, most certainly I have been addled from pain and the wound, but today I woke with clarity. Our situation is most dire."

"Calm yourself, Emma," he whispered, "it is early, barely dawn. Do not wake the entire house. What is wrong?"

"Don't you see? When Henry leaves here people will inquire as to what has happened. Regardless that he shot himself and me, the situation will bring suspicion upon you, and only fuel the fire to his determination to prove you are indeed, John Wilkes Booth. Once Henry recovers, I feel in my heart, he will come after us again."

He agreed, "Yes. He probably will."

"Yes, yes he is still dangerous. You must contact your sister Asia, now, today, right away."

Her fears were making her hysterical, her blue- green eyes wide.

"Yes of course, Emma. I will tell her."

"Please do it today," she urged, frantic to have this handled. "You must tell her what has happened and that we must go into hiding. She will help us. I know she will."

Emma's frantic diatribe had exhausted her again; she fell back against the pillows again, looking fragile and pale. Doing his best to be careful, John sat on the bed, and cradled her into his arms. But still, tears ran down her face as he tried to comfort her fears.

"Dearest Emma," he soothed as he stroked her silken hair. "We cannot go anywhere right now, not until you are stronger. I will contact Asia, but you must rest. You must be strong for our child, our most precious child."

"The baby," she whimpered. "Are you happy?"

John smiled wide, "I cannot tell you of the joy within me at seeing you awake, doubly so with hearing this news. I will admit it humbles me, for I am not worthy of such blessings."

"I disagree. You are very worthy."

With that, she finally laid back comfortably now, her worries placed in his capable hands.

"I must go downstairs to see your mother," John announced his plans, "and tell her of your recovery. She has embraced me as a son. I want to prove her faith in me is not misplaced."

"My family is yours now, husband. In love and in life."

"Yes, it is true."

He stood, turned toward the door, but stopped unable to leave her side without sharing everything on his mind.

"It pains me to know what my heinous deed has done. So much has happened, Emma. So much in so short a time. It feels like a lifetime has been lived in just a few short months. And now because of me, you were shot."

"It wasn't your fault."

"But it was. The bullet that tore through your shoulder was intended to take my life, just like at Garrett's barn when a gunshot felled James William Boyd. Twice I have escaped the hand of sure death. But I fear there will be more attempts. You are correct, the hysteria regarding my identity that began at the hospital in Alexandria has followed us here to Richmond."

"It may follow us, always."

He nodded, even more determined to set things right. "This is not the life I wanted for you, nor the life I intend for our child."

Emma reached up for John's hand and squeezed it. "My husband, please know that I would do nothing different. I gave my body to you freely. My heart you stole the afternoon you arrived at the hospital. I knew then, as I surely know now, that there will never be anyone else for me. Yes, I am now a part of the conspiracy to keep you safe, but I did so willingly. I will never doubt my decision."

"You could have died, Emma."

"But I did not."

"Doctor Hendricks saved you."

"No, love saved me. For the man I fell in love with, the man who took me to his bed, into his heart and his life, was not the same man who committed the crime. For it was love and only love that saved you from malaria. That deadly fever at the hospital nearly killed you."

"Yes, it did."

"But I sat with you, as you have sat here, by my side. My love brought you back. Now, you have done the same for me. You see, I heard your weeping yesterday. Even in the blackness of sleep, I knew you were near. I had to comfort you, dearest husband. That love drew me back, and that is when I awoke to see you."

As he turned to leave, John vowed to do everything in his power to make things right for Emma, for his beautiful and courageous wife, his lovely Mrs. John Singer.

CHAPER SIX

The Dixon Residence in Richmond, Virginia

"I am sure all of these misgivings can be explained away"
~~ Annabelle Dixon

The aftermath of the terrible incident in the Dixon's barn found the house full of an unwanted guest and family. Doctor Hendrix and Old Sam were in a guest room. Henry still remained downstairs, in and out of very deep sleep, his physical wound healing, and his emotional state uncertain. Doctor Hendrix believed he suffered from a severe concussion, in addition to his already delicate mental state. It wasn't so much from the bullet that sliced along his temple, but from when his addled head hit the ground as he fell.

Emma woke late yesterday afternoon and John had been with her nearly non-stop. Annabelle had heard them talking yesterday but did not intrude, they needed and deserved quiet and un-interrupted time to rest and heal.

So very much had happened.

The house servants Esmeralda and Charles were also still asleep. Including herself and Abby, that made eight souls taking haven under her roof. It had actually been a blessing to have company, as if the house welcomed it, providing all the occupants shelter and rest and repose.

Drawing a deep breath as she awoke with the dawn, Annabelle was not used to sleeping alone in the bed she used to share with her beloved husband since his passing. She was fortunate the bed remained intact where so much of the furniture in the house was destroyed. Next to her, Abby was curled up beneath the makeshift covers, her body comfortably warm while she still slept. Her soft golden hair and youthful face were so innocent, so pure.

But Abby had witnessed too much, endured too many upheavals in her young life. Careful not to wake her daughter, Annabelle looked over her shoulder and gazed at her youngest child. After her father and brother were killed in the war, Abby refused to sleep in her own room, instead sleeping with her mother.

Fear and loss had changed Abby. The war had stolen the carefree innocence of her youth. Annabelle sighed as she contemplated the world into which Abigail would forever be entwined. Gone were the days of lovely cotillions and long hot summer nights in fancy dresses, parties and events given to dining and entertaining Richmond's finest families. Gone were her father and brother, never knowing the full joy of their lives.

It was all gone.

Annabelle steadied her thoughts then toward the newest addition to the Dixon household, and that was Emma's husband, John. "How handsome he is," thought Annabelle, "His manners exceptional and his voice melodious. I am sure all of these misgivings can be explained away."

Down the hallway she thought she heard Emma's voice, but then silence ensued. Perhaps she imagined it.

"When things settle I shall speak with John," she decided. "And I sure he can clear up all of this nonsense regarding Henry's fixation about his identity."

After she rose and dressed, the household had many to feed and her worry again passed to the dwindling kitchen foodstuffs. She paused only to bend and kiss the brow of Abigail, who still slept, admiring her beautiful young daughter as she tucked the covers to her chin.

Walking silently down the grand marble staircase that had once been the grandest in all of Richmond, she envisioned her dear husband William, tall and fair haired, waiting at the foot of the stairs his arm extended to welcome her, to join him and host yet another beautiful evening.

She slowly opened her eyes to the reality that was now her existence. The Persian stair runner was stained and torn in various places. The wall covering once the rage in Paris colored in deep burgundy and gold was shadowed by the great pieces of art that once hung in opulence. The bottom step was somehow indented as if by a horseshoe or perhaps a shell.

She slid by the defect unwilling to think more upon it.

It was then she heard a knock upon the door. "How strange," she whispered to herself. The hour so early, not even the house servants were about. Gingerly she opened the door and peered into the early morning sun.

It was her nearest neighbor, a Mrs. Eleanor Morgan, accompanied by her cook Gladys. In their arms were two full baskets. Annabelle's heart leapt with joy at the sight of her kindly neighbor. They had not seen each other for several years, since the time the Dixon house was given to the Confederacy and their generals.

Annabelle had left Richmond with Abigail to reside with relatives in Kentucky after her husband and son were killed. The Morgan family had also fled the entrenched city during the war. She remembered the teary goodbye, not sure if ever the friends would reunite.

Now, here she stood.

"Eleanor, Gladys, oh what a joy this day has brought! Come in, please dear friends, come in. What a blessing to see you once again." Crossing the threshold, Eleanor quickly surveyed the damage the war had inflicted to the foyer and the great staircase. She looked saddened at the state of disrepair, clearly remembering the once opulent home, one of the finest houses in all of Richmond.

But it mattered not for they were reunited.

"I'm so happy our neighbors are finally returning home."

Eleanor smiled at her friend, "My daughter Elisabeth and I only returned to Richmond a few days ago."

"Come, let's visit in here. Everyone is still asleep." Annabelle escorted them past the foyer, and into the parlor.

Eleanor sat gingerly upon the settee and settled her navy dress about her, her dark hair parted in the middle, pulled tight on each side of her face ringlets falling on either side. She was of medium height and the fairest of complexions, but it was her eyes that were the centerpiece of her face, green, bright and piercing. Those eyes focused on her friend as she spoke from her heart.

"Annabelle, I am most sorry for your losses. I heard about your darling husband William and sweet son Caleb."

"Yes, we still feel their loss. We only recently returned, too. Just a few weeks ago, Abby and I were still taking shelter with family in Kentucky."

"Oh Annabelle," sighed Eleanor, "I was astounded and saddened by all I saw. Our city is in ruins. And the people! Our city folk are suffering and starving. I'm sure you heard of our poor suffering city folk. Those who stayed on in Richmond, the times during the war were of desperation and depravity. The bread riots wrought by the women trying to provide for their families. The cost of flour and foodstuffs were so exorbitant, it seemed as if the whole of Richmond was starving."

"After the surrender it was said the burning of Richmond came," Annabelle explained what she knew, "By our own Confederate hands so as not to leave anything for the North. It backfired. The fire raged out of control and I am sure you have seen the results of the devastation."

"Yes, I too sought refuge, "Eleanor explained. " My husband sent me to my family in New York while he stayed and fought." Eleanor's head shook back and forth, "I can't begin to describe the torn alliances I felt with my husband fighting for the Confederacy and my family in New York supporting the Union!"

"Eleanor so much, so very much was torn apart by the war, not just are dear departed soldiers, but families as well."

Eleanor sought to change the mood of the conversation as loss of her husband and son was etched upon Annabelle's face.

"Annabelle, did I mention to you I saw Deacon Burns yesterday when I went to check on our church? I was so pleased to see it still standing. He told me he performed Emma's wedding here, right here! Oh my friend, such joyous news to share with you on this day!"

"Indeed, yes my friend, she is much loved by her John. Our beautiful Emma married a confederate soldier named John Singer. We held the ceremony right here in the front parlor, a short time ago."

Eleanor smiled, "Knowing you had several mouths to feed, and how difficult it is to find food, I thought I should come right away to help." She indicated the baskets that sat on the floor near their feet. "I came to share our supply, for when I left my family's home in New York, they laden me with enough dried meats, fruits and flour enough for weeks. It is more than plenty for my family."

Annabelle's eyes brimmed with tears, "Dear friend," her worry about how to care for everyone under her roof eased, "Your coming here today this very morning is a great blessing. I can only say is an answer to prayers, for our panty in nearly bare. Many are taking refuge in our house."

"You have guests?"

"Yes, an injured physician from Alexandria is here, along with a hospital worker and the head physician of the hospital." She was at that moment reluctant to speak about Henry or the shooting. "Come then let us see to all this glorious food you have brought and leave it for Esmeralda to prepare."

Standing, they quietly made their way toward the kitchen, but heard footsteps on the marble stairs and stopped. Emma's husband John rushed down the stairs. He stopped only to pay his respects to the ladies, his black curly hair falling this way and that in his movements, his black eyes shining. His flawless skin was lightly tanned from time spent in the sun striking against his white cotton shirt. His thigh high black riding boots, shiny and gleaming. He truly looked every bit a dashing gentleman.

John bowed, saying to them, "Good morning, Mother and to your lovely guest. Forgive me, but I must do an errand and will return promptly." He smiled, for the first time in days. "Emma is awake and her coloring is vastly improved. I believe all will be well."

Hearing it made Annabelle happy. "I will see to her, soon."

With that said John raced out.

Eleanor turned to her friend and exclaimed "Who is that very charming and most handsome man?"

Annabelle said simply, "That is Emma's husband, John."

"Has Emma been ill?"

"She had an accident, but it seems she will recover. Come, I will tell you what happened."

"Thank heavens she will recover."

Eleanor and Gladys started to bring the baskets to the Dixon kitchen, but hesitated for a moment as she turned to her friend and said with a shrug, "I think I have seen him before, but I cannot place it."

"Ah well, I'm sure it is of no consequence," interrupted Annabelle, "Come let us bring all of your wonderful food into the kitchen." She recalled what Jonas had said about John and the striking resemblance to John Wilkes Booth. She shook those thoughts and decided to concentrate on the task at hand, and to stop in to see her Emma and find out what was going on.

◆

After Eleanor left, Annabelle had a breakfast tray prepared for Emma and decided to bring it to her. It was tray laden with the goodness of Eleanor's blessings. Fresh baked corn cakes and hot coffee filled the Dixon household with the flavored scents of past abundant times. Annabelle knocked gingerly upon the door of Emma's room, respecting now it was a room occupied by a young husband and wife.

"Emma, may I come in? It is Mother."

A soft voice drifted past the marble threshold as Emma said, "Yes, please come in."

Annabelle stood for a moment before placing the tray on the bedside table. John's chair sat empty, but his side of the bed was rumpled, still bearing the imprint of Emma's handsome husband, his heady masculine scent lingering the room. She then went over to her daughter, carefully surveying her wound, dressed clean and bound tight, her face shining in the morning light.

"Oh Emma, I have been so distraught these last few days. Seeing you awake is a miracle. I am grateful you are well and healing, that is all I care about." She let out a deep sigh. "There is much I need to ask you regarding the past day's events, but the most important thing is that you get well."

She smiled as she caressed her daughter's forehead and fingered a length of her golden hair, the strands like silken ribbon that fell about the pillow behind her.

"I could not bear the thought of losing you." Allowing Emma quiet to eat, she intended to leave. "My questions can wait for another time."

It was a surprise to Annabelle when Emma tugged on her hand in a gesture as to not leave, not yet. She sat on the edge of the bed and waited for Emma to speak. But her chin moved in soundless motions as she struggled to find words.

"What is it, dear? You can tell me."

"Oh Mother," cried out Emma, "I want to tell you something important, but I am not sure of how you will react."

She lowered her head.

"Emma look at me," Annabelle cajoled. "Don't you know there is nothing you can do or say that will ever change my love for you, do you understand?"

Emma nodded her head and whispered, "I am with child. I was with child when I went to the altar, having been with John some months before."

"Tell me Emma, tell me what is going on."

"Please Mother, understand the love I have for him, it's stronger than the life within me." Emma reminisced, "You see from the very first time I laid eyes on him, it was like nothing and no one else existed, that my life was somehow intertwined with his, forever. When he told me he loved me and wished to marry, I broke the promises of womanhood and lay with him before we went to the altar. It was, I believe when the child was conceived. Forgive me Mother for this, but I cannot ask forgiveness for the love I have for John nor do I want to change anything."

Emma's eyes filled with tears, her chin had lowered to her chest with this last heartfelt confession of love, afraid of what her mother would say.

Annabelle's heart lurched at her daughter's news. The need for rest and healing taking on a greater meaning now as the news of her expectant grandchild resonated in her heart and mind. She placed her hand under Emma's chin and lifted her face to meet hers.

"I meant it. You should know, there is nothing you could do or say to change my love for you. This war has taken so much, but it has given us much as well." She smiled wide, "Oh, this is joyful news. A child, yours and John's. My grandchild."

"But, I thought you would be upset, especially knowing the truth about when the baby was conceived. It was not within the sacred bonds of marriage, yet."

"Yes, we both know as women the lot we bear for what we do for love and how one wrong turn can forever destroy a woman's chances for a good and decent life. But war changes everything. It is important to know that when you find love, hold on with your heart and with both hands. That you and John acted on your love before the altar is truly between both you two. I cannot say more to this. But child, I know of love and the power of it, and what it can do to a woman's sensibilities. We are told by our mothers to be prepared for the marriage bed, and instructed of the awful temptation of love before marriage."

She shook her head as she remembered the yearnings of physical love shared with her own husband, the comfort and intimacy something Annabelle missed in the years since his death.

Unexpectedly, her mind flashed to the kind Doctor Hendrix, asleep down the hall. She pondered their recent conversation for a moment and thought of his kindness and generosity towards her and her family.

"Now eat Emma, and rest and heal not only for yourself, but to take care of the precious child within you."

"Thank you, Mother, for understanding."

"I suspect our Doctor needs to be made aware of your condition, so he can properly address your future care." She turned to leave. "We must not delay for Jonas leaves today for Alexandria."

"Mother," asked Emma incredulously, "Such familiarity with Doctor Hendrix?"

Annabelle smiled a sly slight smile before closing the door lightly behind her, "Indeed."

━━━━━━ ◆ ━━━━━━

Emma ate her breakfast and then lay back against the pillow. Her heart ached, knowing the urgency of John's errand at this early hour was to find the dispatch office in Richmond and send word to sister Asia of the attack by Henry and to ask her help.

Emma thoughts wandered briefly as she remembered John's words in their intense discussion this morning.

He knelt down beside her and took her hand as they talked about the urgency of their situation. His identity must be protected, at all costs.

"We will find safety from Henry," her husband had assured. "I just have to find the dispatch office and send word to sister Asia of what has happened here."

Knowing he was taking action eased some of her fears.

"Once he recovers," she felt adamant, "it will be as it was before, his ranting and railing against you. We cannot risk even the slightest chance he could find anyone to believe his claims."

"I know, what he needs for proof."

John then reached from inside his shirt and pulled out the small red diary. As he opened it, the folded news clipping scattered across her lap, the WANTED poster and also the letter to Asia that Emma had found and used in secret to guide her to his sister's home in Philadelphia.

If Emma had found it and used it, so to could anyone else if the diary was in the wrong hands.

"This is what he wants. This, and me dead."

Emma then begged of her husband, "John please just burn it, please!"

John saw the pain and worry in Emma's beautiful eyes and wanted nothing more than to grant her desire for he knew she was right, but instead he signed deeply and said to her, "Emma, I cannot burn this, for inasmuch it is proof of evidence of who I truly am and the crime I committed, I cannot let it go."

"Although it is dangerous to hold onto it, if I did it burn it, the act for me would seem as if by burning it I could erase all that I have done. Nothing will change that. It is a reminder for me no matter where I go or where I hide, I can never escape my past."

With that said John left Emma's side and hurried to the dispatch office. There was no time to waste.

❖

The clanging of pots and pans in a nearby kitchen and the rich scent of coffee woke Henry from his restless sleep. His head was pounding furiously, the darkened small room unfamiliar to him as he tried to rouse himself to a seated position on the small narrow bed.

He searched his thoughts that seemed muddled, at best. His memories were large gaps of time. He finally remembered what he had done, why he lay bandaged and alone in the small room. It tore through him, the lost memories returning in a rush as the horror of hurting Emma riveted him to the core. He recalled in painful detail the moment the derringer rose to kill John and suddenly Emma had jumped in front of her husband.

The bullet meant for John, finding its way to her lush and beautiful body. He searched his mind remembering reloading the single shot derringer once again, not aiming at John, but rather his own head, he did not understand why he was still alive, and after all he killed his love Emma, shot her dead.

There was nothing left to live for now.

He drew in a deep breath of pain as he drew his hand to the side of his head, and he felt the bandage that now was crusted with his dried blood.

The tears fell from his eyes and left soft pools of moisture upon the well-worn sheet that covered him and laid his aching head back and then remembered what he thought was a dream. He forced his foggy thoughts to recall the night, his darkened room, and his late night visitor.

Henry searched his aching head for recognition, until he knew the shadowy figure. The dark evil shadows had crept around his room. He also remembered the half smile upon the man's face as he left the room and Henry called out to him, "Booth." All at once he suddenly remembered where he was.

Emma's house.

A place he had frequented as a youth and young man many times growing up in Richmond prewar society. The pain suddenly became fierce, the room began to spin, as he called out, "Please come! Please help me." Henry laid his head back for what seemed a moment or two when the door opened to the familiar face and figure that was of Doctor Jonas Hendrix.

"Henry," he cried, "You are awake."

"Yes, it was just a very bad flesh wound, you will be well, you gave us quite a scare!"

"Old Sam and I will be taking you to your parents' house later today."

"Oh Henry, I am so sorry this all happened."

"Too much suffering Henry after four long years and now this!"

He bowed his head and shook it several times as Henry cried to him, "You should not have saved me Jonas, should have let me bled out there and die, I killed my Emma I killed her! You see," he confessed, "I came here to kill John. He is Booth, I just know it, Jonas. Why he crept into my room under the dark of night and practically admitted it!"

"But I killed my Emma and he lives!"

His heart lurched thinking the breath in his lungs should be snuffed out, just like Emma's.

"Henry, listen to me. Emma is fine, just a shoulder wound she is young and strong. She just needs to eat and rest, is all."

Henry roused his head and stared into the exhausted physician's eyes and said incredulously, "She is alive, my Emma is alive?"

"Yes, she is alive. Now you must not excite yourself. We will be preparing to leave soon. Old Sam," called Doctor Hendrix though the open bedroom door. "Are you there?"

The meager sunlight filtering from the kitchen into the small bedroom was diminished as the great hulking form of Old Sam filled its threshold. "Yes'um Doc, I is here, I is here."

He walked over to the bed where his friend laid, the life in his eyes struggling to focus and he knelt before the bed. "You gave Old Sam here quite a scare when you done took off after Mr. John and Miss Emma, that day. Me and Doc Hendrix done followed you just in time, we saw Mr. John taking Miss Emma into the house, her front all bloody, just like so many soldiers we done seen at the hospital."

"But thanking God, she will recover, right?"

"Yes Sir, she is good. But I then found you in the stable your life flowing out of you, I thought you'se was dead. But you was alive. It was Doc Hendrix who done saved your life. I begged God to spare your life, and so He did. So now, I ain't ever leavin' your side, ever."

The large man held his gaze until Henry's mind absorbed the words and he nodded in understanding.

"I jest don't understand this Henry, how could you try to kill Mr. John? All the killin' and all the dying we done seen, and now you was aiming to kill to? And where'd you git that gun? I ain't ever seen it before."

"Old Sam," he whispered, "Devoted friend Old Sam, what shall I do? My Emma is married to Booth, I just know it is him. You saw the diary. I know there is evidence I know in that diary. I am going to get it. Once I have it, I can take it to Washington as proof. It's either by my hand he will die Sam, or with the wrath of the government upon him."

Henry nodded his head up and down as he ranted his plan.

"I must find that diary I must!" he ranted over and over, "I must and you will help me right Old Sam, you will!"

Old Sam reached out to touch the hand of his friend, laying his oversized hand over the Doctor's shaking slim hand and squeezed it.

He then said to his friend, "Doc Hendrix seys all youse need to do is to rest and let your wound heal. All this other talk is for another day, just know Old Sam is never letting you outta my sight, ever, where you go I go. Doc Hendrix says we are going to take to you to your mammy and pappy's house to rest there. This here is Emma and Mister John's house. It's no place for us now. It's best we take leave, the sooner the better."

"Old Sam," begged Henry, his mind stuck on the one detail he felt sure would bring about vindication. "Don't let them get away with that diary. It's proof Singer is really Booth. You must help me get it." Pains shot through his temple, radiating across his brow. Once again, the dark curtains of reality were closing around him. Henry's body felt limp in the bed.

"But right now my head is pounding. And I am so very very tired." With that said Henry laid his head back and fell back to sleep.

Doctor Hendrix checked the wound once again and as he finished his inspection turned to Old Sam, "As soon as he is awake and fed, we will take him to his parents. We must get him away from this house and John and Emma, for everyone's sake!"

Old Sam could only nod his head and mutter, "Yes suh!"

CHAPTER SEVEN

Field Hospital in Alexandria, Virginia

"No, it cannot be true, Henry what have you done?'
~~Louisa May Alcott

At the hospital, it was while Louisa was tidying up in Henry's room that she heard a noise outside the front door. She had tried to stay busy, walking in and out of the rooms these last few days to do whatever needed to be done to keep everything running, all the while she was wringing her hands with worry while waiting to hear from him or Doctor Hendrix.

She glanced into his bedroom as she walked by and saw a pile of clothes strewn upon the floor and a chair under the only window in the room. She lowered her eyes to that sight realizing it was through this window that Henry had eluded Old Sam.

She just prayed whatever happened, it would not be another death to bear on her heart.

John Singer and the former nurse Emma Dixon had to gone to Richmond to start a new life together. It left Henry distraught over the marriage, compounded by his insistence that John Singer was really John Wilkes Booth, the assassin of President Lincoln. It had overwhelmed his exhausted mind.

Rushing to open the door in hopes the sound she heard was Henry returning, Louisa found instead the stable boy Isaac. He handed her a letter.

"Oh, thank God. We have news at last. Thank you, Isaac."

"You're welcome, Miss Louisa," responded the young stable boy, "I hope you get good news. But I best be getting back, them stable horses will be wondering where I is."

Louisa returned to Henry's room and sat upon the couch. Her hands were shaking as she tore at the envelope to reveal the message. Her fears were heightened as she read the words that were incredulous to her.

Dear Miss Alcott:

It is with the deepest regret I tell you of the most grievous circumstances that have befallen our Henry and Emma.

Old Sam and I arrived too late to stop Henry from doing harm. He had cornered John in the stable at Emma's home here in Richmond. He tried to shoot him, but in defense of her husband John, the bullet hit our beautiful Emma in her shoulder instead. She will recover I am thankful to God for that. Oh Miss Alcott, how wrong we were to believe this war was over, when in fact the damage it wrought still rages in the defeated minds of those we care so deeply about!

Henry was unable to let go of his unrequited feelings for Emma, but I never saw this violence coming, not like this. And this talk of John being in fact John Wilkes Booth! Such nonsense this diatribe is, but so dangerous in these most perilous of times.

Old Sam and I arrived just a moment too late, unable to stop Henry. Believing he killed Emma, he tried to commit suicide. But God is not finished with him, for the bullet merely grazed his head. He too, will recover.

We are taking Henry back to his family's house here in Richmond. His head wound, although painful will heal, but he still suffers from erratic emotional outbursts and effects from a concussion.

Henry must be watched carefully. I cannot stay any longer. I have duties and responsibilities in Alexandria. But I am grateful he is not alone. Old Sam cannot be moved from Henry's side, going so far as to sleep on the floor next to his bed to help secure his recovery. And Henry's parents are here and grievously concerned for their son.

I hope I do not ask too much of you. Please consider taking the train to Richmond to visit. As a dear friend to both Emma and Henry, I thought it best to inform you what has befallen our dear friends, and the ones who love them so very much, as well.

I remain most respectfully,
Jonas Hendrix, MD

Louisa still grasped the letter with both hands, the tears of pain and sadness for her friends falling like a gentle drops of rain upon the words that now blurred under her sight.

"Oh Henry," she lamented, "What have you done?"

She stood and walked to the door, still trying to understand the events that had stung her heart. "Yes," she murmured to herself, "I will travel to Richmond. I must do this, to help as best I can."

She stood there for an additional moment recalling Henry's crazed ranting about John Singer, how he believed the handsome soldier was really John Wilkes Booth. She refused to participate in Henry's delusions. She was sure there was a reasonable explanation.

As she hurried from Henry's place, there was one stop she intended to make before packing and sending a telegraph advising Doctor Hendrix that she would come to visit, and that was to see her dear friend Walt.

His worry over their friends was worn like etched glass through his kind face. She remembered the bantering of Henry and Walt, as the young and the old finding favor with the work and care they both provided to the suffering soldiers these four long years.

Louisa hastened her step, as she decided to not only tell Walt all of the terrible news from Richmond; she also hoped to convince him to come with her.

She found Walt in the one area of the hospital that would remain open, the section for those poor soldiers who were too sick or injured to be moved.

Most of the ambulatory patients had been released now that the war was over. But Louisa shook her head as she thought of the many men that were going home without arms, legs, to an uncertain future, some unable to provide for their families.

She then spied the kind-hearted poet by the all too familiar bedside of a dying soldier, helping the man pen a letter to a loved one at home.

Louisa waited at the doorway of the room until he finished, not willing to disturb the precious words from a dying loved one. She watched as Walt touched the hand of the young soldier and stood up only then seeing Louisa at the doorway. He smiled then and walked towards her.

The poet extended his hand to Louisa but as he saw her worried expression, the smile disappeared from his face, "You have news, Miss Louisa?" He waited as Louisa extended her hand and opened it to reveal the letter from Doctor Hendrix. Walt lowered his eyes, shook his head and murmured to Louisa, "I cannot look upon it for I know it bears unhappy news, tell me please. But let's go outside first before you speak."

Louisa followed Walt and they both sat upon the bench where just a short time ago they had found Henry after his encounter with John Singer, his ranting causing them both great fear for his safety. Walt turned towards her, his eyes already welling up with emotion in anticipation of the difficult news folded his hands upon his lap and waited for her to speak.

"Oh Walt, the news is difficult to bear, but know no matter what I tell you, please know both Henry and Emma will recover." Louisa took a deep breath as she allowed him time to read the letter from Jonas, recounting the terrible events.

Louisa watched as the tears stemmed from her friend's eyes, eyes that had seen too much death, too much suffering. Now those tears were shed for the Doctor and dear friend who had struggled for four long years of the war to stop that death.

"Walt, as you know, Henry saved my life, calling me back from the blackness of pain and suffering from losing my love, Jack. He brought me back to the living. I cannot abandon him in his hour of need. Clearly, he needs help to guide him past his obsession with Emma and John."

"Yes, he does."

"Our good Doctor Hendricks cannot shoulder this burden alone. Henry's misguided affections are destructive and must cease. And poor Emma, she deserves none of this."

Walt nodded, "No she certainly does not."

"I ask if perhaps you would accompany me to Richmond, and help ease the pain of so many affected by Henry's act?"

The old man blinked, his red rimmed eyes brimming with the stain of so much grief and managed through a hoarse voice, "Yes, Miss Louisa, I will go with you."

He then raised himself slowly from the bench and walked back to his place to pack, his shoulders stooped with the weight of what was yet to come.

CHAPTER EIGHT

The Dixon Residence in Richmond, Virginia

"It is with much regret I must take my leave of you"
~~ Jonas Hendrix, MD

It was still early in the morning and Doc Hendrix had tended both Henry and Emma to his satisfaction. After Henry's crazed outburst, he could not delay. He sought out Annabelle to tell her he was taking Henry that very morning to his parents' house and asked her for guidance and directions to his boyhood home.

He was told of Emma's forthcoming child. His examination of her confirmed the presence of an infant. He cautioned Emma that since there was blood loss from her wound, eating and resting was imperative for both mother and child.

It was just as he had stepped into the parlor that Annabelle joined him. "So Jonas," queried Mrs. Dixon, "You will be definitely leaving us today to take Henry home?"

Jonas admired her loveliness. In that moment the wish for someone to love and hold felt overwhelming to him as he said sadly, "Yes Annabelle, I am taking Henry away. His mind is still not right. He still burns with much ill guided emotions. It is best to remove him as soon as possible far away from John and Emma."

She nodded to agree.

"It is with much regret that I must take my leave of you. I have written to Henry's good friend from the hospital, Miss Louisa May Alcott, asking her to come visit with Henry."

"Perhaps that will help him."

"Be assured however, that I will return here to your home to see to our Emma and her child and Henry also, but also I most certainly hope, to come to call on you."

Annabelle smiled, "I should be sorely disappointed if you did not." With that she extended her hand to him, but rather than taking her hand to his lips he boldly stepped forward and lightly kissed her lovely cheek.

It was a bold and startling gesture. She did not admonish him. Annabelle lowered her gaze and moved closer still to Jonas. It was if the universe had silently given them a blessing as much to her surprise Annabelle moved closer still and dropped her weary head upon Jonas' shoulder.

The brief comfort provided a respite from so much loss and suffering as she felt his arms embrace her. As quickly as the moment had arisen it ended however, as Jonas suddenly broke his embrace and started for the parlor door. He turned long enough to see a slight tear falling from her startling blue eyes, the sight of which tore at his aching heart.

Reluctant to leave, he forced himself to go. He then found Old Sam waiting for him in the foyer as he heard the soft spoken hulking man say to him, "I done got the Dixon carriage all ready for Henry, that old nag of a carriage horse has just enough left in her to get us there. I done seen your horse that Henry stole too, Doc. He's in the barn, I done give him hay and water."

Old Sam made his way to the back bedroom off of the kitchen fully prepared to carry his friend into the waiting carriage. He didn't allow Jonas to help. He insisted on caring for Henry, alone.

It was while he was carrying Henry through the house that he suddenly stopped in his tracks, seeing John hurry through the front door, fresh from his morning errand.

"We be leavin' now, Mister John."

John stood motionless as he watched Henry's faithful friend carry him across the foyer. For a few seconds that Henry was able to focus his eyes on John, the fury build up in him lashing out in a tirade. "Booth! I know it's you. I almost killed my Emma with a bullet meant to pierce your black heart. Mark my words, I will have vengeance."

John stood motionless listening, yet could not help adding more fuel to Henry's ire. He moved close to his face, John's voice even and menacing. "Ah for sure you think I am Booth? Good luck trying to prove it. No one will believe you. Rant all you like, but in the end you will end up dead yourself for the insidious delusions you are so very sure about. Emma is mine, and that baby is mine. You will never have her, ever."

"A baby, a baby," cried out Henry, "No it cannot be true."

"Yes, she is due in December."

"That baby should have been mine!"

Upon hearing that John tossed back his head, his black shiny curls falling free. "Never. Emma could never love you!"

He was still laughing as Old Sam raced past him, putting Henry inside the waiting carriage.

John closed the front door and turned suddenly then to run and check on Emma when he saw Doctor Hendrix moving towards him. He apparently heard everything.

"I don't know who you are or are pretending to be. It is none of my business, but what is my business is that sweet expectant mother upstairs and the wellbeing of my best surgeon. You should not have told Henry about the baby in his fragile condition."

"He needs to know the truth."

"Yet, I am not sure what is going on here." He examined John more closely. "Yes so as I look at your face, I do see the resemblance to pictures I have seen of John Wilkes Booth, and it is very striking. Stay away from Henry, Mr. Singer. Or should I say, Booth?”

John gritted his teeth and said icily, “My Name is John Singer,”

“So you claim.”

“Emma is Mrs. John Singer and she loves me. It is a fact Henry would be wise to remember.”

“Wise. Is anyone wise, anymore? I believe wisdom died when someone put a bullet in our good President.”

Jonas then shook his head, and took leave of John and made his way into the carriage. He could only stand there motionless once again. The menacing laughter he enjoyed just a few moments ago lost in the Doctor’s parting words.

———— ◆ ————

The clip clop of the Dixon horse was the only sound on the broken road from the Dixon residence to the Bradley residence just a few miles away. Inside the once resplendent carriage now worn down from soldiers use during the war, Doctor Hendrix rode with his patient Henry Bradley leaning on him for support. The once besotted bandage around Henry’s head was no longer speckled with blood. The wound was healing. Jonas peered out from the curtain less window, his eyes slowly awakening to the complete ravages of the once beautiful city.

The rows of stately homes from the Dixon residence forward were in varying degrees of destruction. Some had no roofs, other no walls; some were just the remains of a once grand fireplace chimney, a singular stoic reminder of the past glory of the wealthier citizens of Richmond.

He would on occasion see a resident or two wander out from one of the many broken homes as if recognizing the once resplendent carriage, follow it with their saddened eyes and retreat back into the shadows of what once was. Jonas could only hope that time with Henry’s parents would heal his physical and emotional wounds.

Yet, he was not sure of this nor was he even sure Henry would recover emotionally; his outburst at seeing John in those few moments before they left reinforced this deep seated hatred of each other.

He thought then of what he had said to John in those moments, John’s cruelty at telling Henry of the baby and the menacing laughter John had expressed at Henry’s obvious pain.

He decided then he would speak to Old Sam about this diary that was rumored held some sort of supposed evidence that points to the notion that John Singer was really John Wilkes Booth.

Jonas' close workings with Henry in the four long years at the field hospital in Alexandria proved to him that Henry was not only an extremely talented surgeon, but one who had deep compassion and empathy.

That Henry believed so deeply in John's supposed deception made Jonas uneasy and seeing his reaction to him earlier in the day only sought to solidify that feeling. He could only shake his head and hold Henry close as the deeply riveted road jolted them causing the occupants of the carriage to be tossed about.

———————◆———————

Meanwhile in Philadelphia, the young mother grasped her infant to her breast, the tufts of black hair felt like glossy silk against her palm. Asia walked the floor of her large bedroom with her infant son, the sound of his cooing soothing the young mother's heart. She still could not believe her own eyes as she remembered the sight of the life and body of her dear brother John's incredible escape to freedom and the soulful agonizing look in his deep penetrating eyes. She had left her home and children to go with a woman who had darkened her door, a stranger then, only to be told her beloved brother was alive and the beautiful brave woman was his wife. It was too much.

Her husband John Sleeper Clarke had been released from prison several days ago. Thankfully, Asia had arrived back from Richmond prior to her husband's release. Her trip was kept silent by those in the Clarke household, all being sworn to keep secret of Asia's departure from Philadelphia with the beautiful young woman who had boldly visited, bringing news of her brother.

She could not tell her husband anything due to distinct animosity that had always existed between the two men, that fact reminiscent on her wedding day when John told her not to marry the man, as the Booth name was indeed a plum dowry for one who managed and owned theaters.

Asia could only bow her head as she realized and admitted he was indeed right.

The baby's cooing sounds were dispelled as Jacob and Joshua rushed into their mother's bedroom, their footsteps pounding on the shiny hardwood floor. Both boys were out of breath, their faces bright with excitement. Jacob pulled on her skirt, anxious to be heard.

"Yes child, what is it?" asked Asia, one arm cuddling her infant the other running over the handsome cheek of her oldest boy. At five years old, he was full of energy. With each passing day the resemblance between him and his Uncle was like an identical twin.

"Mama," began Jacob, "I was telling Joshua you went to find Uncle John he doesn't believe me. He says it's not so. "Tell him, Mama. That you and me both heard Uncle John calling us to come find him. You left with that pretty lady. Did you find him?"

Jacob's insistence was too much for the young mother's heart, the forbidden knowledge that her brother John was alive and the burdens to not only keep the secret, but to somehow keep him alive were too much to think about at that moment. There was so much at stake, not just John's life but his wife's and her entire family and children as well.

Asia went to the small crib and placed the sleepy baby in the cradle. She waited until the tug of sleep weighed down the infant's dark eyes.

"Boys," she whispered, "Let us go down to the front parlor. We don't want to wake baby John."

Both Jacob and Joshua smiled at their mother's mention of the infant's name. They knew the child's name was supposed to be Joseph after their Uncle, but the deep and abiding love of and promise made to their Uncle John to name the child if a boy after him changed as she secretly named him John Joseph and shared that fact with her older boys.

Asia followed them downstairs. She sat on the edge of the long ornate sofa and held out her hands to both her boys. Jacob and Joshua ran to their mother and then sat at her feet as she lowered her hands as to see them face to face.

"Boys listen to me, listen very carefully and just like the secret we have that baby Joseph's name is really John Joseph, what I am about to tell you, you must lock into your hearts and never ever repeat this to no one do you understand no one except me. Do you swear to this?"

The boys nodded their heads in acknowledgement, then crying out, "We promise."

"Boys, listen carefully. You remember not too long ago the pretty lady that came here and stayed with us for one night? Then I left you both and went with her."

"I remember," Jacob chimed in.

"Her name is Emma. She had information about your Uncle John." Asia took a deep breath as she continued, "Boys, she took me to see our Uncle John. He is alive, I saw him!"

"Where is he, "Both boys shouted in unison, where is Uncle John?"

"Please tell us Mama, please tell us!"

"He is in Richmond, living there with his wife Emma. He is called John Singer, now. I know how much you love him. I wanted you to know. I know how hurt and confused you have both felt, these past months. But you must keep our secret. It is very dangerous for anyone else to know."

It was Jacob who suddenly sprang to his feet, the dark stare narrowing as he asked his mother, "Mama does Papa know this?"

Asia met his gaze intent on the child's face and simply said, "No child, he does not."

Asia only then realized she was crying as her oldest son reached to wipe away her tears. He was no longer an innocent carefree boy. He was becoming aware of the bad in the world.

"Mama, we won't tell."

It was the middle boy Joshua who then asked, "Mama will we get to see Uncle John, will we?"

"Child," she responded, "I don't honestly know. Right now I must contact your Uncle Edwin and bring him to Philadelphia."

Jacob silent for the moment, turned his noble young face to his mother and asked, "Mama, why is Uncle John, John Singer?"

"I don't understand. Is it because everyone is mad at Uncle John and that he did something bad like the newspapers say all the time?'

Asia stroked the jet black curls of her oldest son, and tried to ease his mind. "Jacob, please don't worry about such things, the most important is that we are family and family helps and protects each other."

It was just after she had spoken these words that the doorbell clanged. She heard Mrs. McLeary answer the door, and then came to the parlor with a letter in her hand. The house servant bowed as she handed it to the mistress of the house.

Smiling, the servant said to the two small boys, "I think there is some sweet cake in the kitchen. Maybe you boys could help me find it."

Jacob and Joshua looked at their mother, waiting for permission to leave. Asia nodded her head in appreciation of Mrs. McLeary's care of the boys and sat back down upon the ornate couch to read the letter. Her hands were shaking as she noticed the familiar handwriting of her brother, John. She had just left him several days ago, the worry and fear of his situation causing her hands to shake as she read his words.

Dearest sister mine,
It is with a heavy heart I tell you of the most grievous things that have befallen Emma and I since you left us just these two weeks past. Remember we told you there was someone who was so

incredulous and addled as to his belief that indeed I am Booth and equally incredulous that Emma should have taken me for her husband and not this addled Doctor Bradley a former surgeon at the field hospital in Alexandria.

Oh Asia, he followed us here to Richmond and cornered me in the stable his derringer aimed at my heart, he was convinced I was Booth, and that I must die for the crime I committed and that he would take Emma after I was gone, convincing her he was the better man.

He raised the derringer to fire, then Emma came into the stable, having been calling for me. She stepped in front of the derringer and it hit her in the shoulder! I took her then into the house, just as I did I heard the gun cock again and watched as that fool aimed the gun at his head and fired! I saw only my Emma as I raced into the house, meeting the head of the hospital Jonas Hendrix riding furiously up to the house, followed by Doctor Bradley's faithful friend and hospital worker Old Sam.

They had been following after that fool Bradley knowing his addled brain and insidious accusations. God has once again favored me, for this reason I still do not understand, but I am forever grateful for his gifts as the wound to Emma was not fatal, and although there was blood loss, her youth and energy will sustain her to a complete recovery. Added to that favor from God, dear sister is the news that my Emma is with child. We should expect this child perhaps at Christmastime.

You should also know that the self-inflicted wound to Henry was not fatal; the bullet grazed the temple not through it unfortunately. He is being tended to by Doctor Hendrix and is being removed today to his family's house somewhere here in Richmond.

He wants me dead Asia, that and my diary as proof against my glommed identity of John Singer. His ranting and close proximity to Emma and I have me gravely concerned for Emma and our child. I ask of you then to make haste to contact the family, and bring them and mother to Tudor Hall. I will come with Emma under the guise of night and announce myself to our dear mother. Emma needs much rest now as the need for her to rest and heal is greater now with the start of child. I will look to come to Tudor Hall in early July.

My duty now is to my wife and child and their health and safety; I owe Emma and you everything. Dearest sister, forgive me please. Know that my heart and love of you and the boys is with me always. Kiss Jacob for me.

Johnny

Asia clasped the letter to her heart and rocked back and forth on the couch as if trying to dispel the terrible words written by her brother. The suffering of all involved at the Dixon house tore at her as she agonized over the terrible event. She pictured Emma lunging in front of John, mistakenly taking the bullet that was meant for him. Emma's instinct to protect her husband was an unselfish act.

She knew how much Emma loved John and felt she was very brave to come find her. John did not know of Emma's deception and his new wife risked it all to bring Asia and John together.

She was a remarkable woman. She thought then for a moment of John's news of a child, "My Johnny. A father! Oh what a life this child is entering into!"

A life on the run, in denial of his/her heritage, forever bound by the dark secret of their father's great crime. As she thought of John's great love of her own children, she knew exactly how he would react to this child, his child. He would be fiercely protective and grateful for the new life that God had blessed him with.

Asia deeply believed that the love of child sometimes comes with great sacrifice. She wondered if John understood. He may be called to give his greatest gift yet, not just his heart, but perhaps his very own life to prove his love to his child.

Standing, she straightened her dress, wiped the tears from her face as she walked by the foyer mirror. She went to the kitchen to check on the boys, but she stopped for a moment at the serious reflection staring back at her.

Her deep-set dark eyes looked soulful as they reflected the pain in her heart. Her dark hair was kept braided and twisted about her head like a crown, her skin the same white alabaster like her brother John. For as handsome as he was, so too was she as beautiful.

The days of growing up at Tudor Hall skated through her mind, reflecting back upon better and happier times. She reminisced of the days of climbing the great cherry tree in front of the house, and resting on one of the large shady branches that moved out from the tree like so many numerous arms. Arms that held the many Booth children that sought refuge in the great tree on many sultry summers Maryland afternoons while they swung with merriment from its large branches.

Asia remembered one sultry afternoon in particular, once in which her brother John exclaimed to her, "Isn't just delicious to breathe?" His remark was an effort to dispel her sulking, and so he did as he always did with his gallant and sweet disposition.

She ran her hands across her smooth high cheeks and moved away from the mirror determined above all to protect her brother and his family, all at once not knowing how this could be done.

CHAPTER NINE

The Bradley Residence in Richmond, Virginia

"I must get word to Sergeant Beau Jackson,
he will help me"
~~ Henry Bradley

The comfort of the down feather pillow behind Henry's aching head felt vaguely familiar. He opened his eyes and focused on the room where he rested. It was his boyhood bedroom in Richmond.

His gaze followed the sunlight coming through the three large floor to ceiling windows, across from his bed. The late morning light shone through bare windows, empty now of any coverings.

He looked at the light blue Persian carpet and noticed its stained and torn areas. The large wardrobe that covered the opposite side of the windows was open with hand carved cherrywood doors laid wide to reveal the inside, silently bearing to its occupant to witness the emptiness within.

What happened here?

He had left here only four years ago. His parent's home was one that had rivaled the Dixon's grand home.

He vaguely remembered his flight into Richmond and the chimneys that littered the streets, remembering now that was all that stood from the burning of the city in the war, some months ago. His parents were some of the lucky ones.

But what of the rest of the house? How much of it is still standing?

His mind confused and his head aching, he only distantly remembered his recent exodus from the Dixon house while cradled in the arms of his friend Old Sam, and the unplanned meeting of John Singer in the foyer as they exited the house.

Henry's ire grew as he remembered the words of his adversary haunting and taunting him as he lay helpless in Old Sam's arms.

A child, thought Henry.

No, this cannot be.

Emma is with child, he agonized, Booth's child.

"I know now what I must do." He muttered to himself. "I am not addled. Is it really so crazy to try to prove to the country they killed the wrong man in Garrett's barn? The real killer is living right under their nose in Richmond, but they will want proof in Washington."

Henry knew to ask Old Sam about the diary, for he was aware of it and had described its contents. John and Emma must still have it. For as canny as this John Singer is, he as Booth would not burn or destroy the only one true vestige of his identity.

"And so, what then of Emma?" He continued his private mutterings. "She must know of his identity."

But how could it be that this most perfect woman of whom he idolized could have been so blinded as to have married this murderer and would continue to hide under the guise of John Singer? It was not possible.

He had worked with Emma for years at the hospital. He remembered the thousands of soldiers she tended, had seen so much suffering, yet for many men only seeing her beautiful face was the last sight for their eyes, as death came swift for so many of them.

Henry sighed as he thought of all that had happened since the appearance of John Singer in Alexandria. His luck that the broken leg had no gangrene, his bout with malaria and his recovery. His romance with Emma and leaving with her, coming to Richmond.

To be married.

That tormented him too.

Oh, how he hated John.

He then remembered his patient, Beau Jackson, the one soldier who gave Henry a derringer as a way of saying thanks for saving his life. Remembering too the man's carefully calculated words, "Some people just need killin.'"

Beau's bed in the hospital had been beside John Singer's. The two men had talked enough for Beau to decide John was not a friend, but foe.

Henry would need help finding the diary that would convince the men in Washington that John Wilkes Booth still lived. But who would help him? Who wanted John Singer dead as much as he did?

He lay there for a long time, staring at the ceiling of his bedroom, his thoughts filled with hateful vengeance.

"Why Sergeant Beau Jackson of course," he finally muttered to himself as his mind cleared. "Jackson saw through Singer's guise, hated him." That realization got his blood stirring. "I will find a way to get word to him."

Henry thought again for a while, vaguely remembered Old Sam mentioning he was originally from the same town in North Carolina as Sergeant Jackson.

"I will find way to get word to him. He will help me, I know it!" His spluttered words went unheard, except by the bedroom walls. He then rested his head on the down pillows as the pain from his temple throbbed and exploded in pain.

"I must now step easy," connived Henry, "I must convince all of my repentance for all I have wrought and feign a multitude of apologies. I must do this now, yet stay steadfast in my deception. Only by being convincing all of my errant ways will I be able to reach out to Sergeant Jackson tell him what is truly happening and ask him to come to Richmond."

That felt like a solid plan.

"Then together we will hunt down Booth, take the diary and bring it to Washington and then Emma will be mine."

Henry heard a soft knocking upon his door and the voice of Doctor Hendrix asked, "Henry may I come in?"

Henry raised his throbbing head and called out, "Yes of course Jonas, please come in."

He watched as Jonas walked to his bedside, his face lined and etched with worry. Only a man in his early fifties, the war had added additional years to his countenance, making him appear much older than he was.

Henry knew he had to convince Jonas he was repentant and that his previous behavior was all a horrible mistake. He would be tested and questioned many, many times as to his veracity and his sudden and deeply apologetic beliefs, yet he must convince Jonas in particular, in order to secretly conspire to move forward with his plans.

"Henry," began Jonas, "Old Sam and I have brought you back to your parent's house here in Richmond to recover and rest. I am speechless as to the events of the last few days. I am so sorry I was not more aware of your pain as to the situation with Emma. I thought it was the effects of exhaustion and the unspeakable things we saw from that terrible war."

The Doctor sighed and sat beside Henry's bed. "While we were in Alexandria, your friend Miss Alcott came and spoke to me of your unrequited feelings for Emma." He swallowed, meeting Henry's gaze solidly. "She loves you. Miss Alcott was so worried about you. She cares very much. As we all do."

"I am grateful for her concern." Henry replied, trying to look contrite and repentant.

"But Henry, this ranting about John Singer actually being Booth has to stop. Perhaps he does resemble him and his actions are questionable, but he is married to Emma now and she is with child. It is only through the goodness and friendship with Mrs. Dixon that no charges will be sought against you for trying to kill John."

"I am fortunate."

"You are fortunate indeed. But it changes nothing if you continue to rant and threaten John and Emma. And this diary I have heard so much about, the one found by Emma and Old Sam back in Alexandria, so what if it contained news clippings and wanted posters. What does that really prove? Nothing."

"No, I suppose not." But saying the words felt bitter and false against Henry's tongue.

"Be reminded," said Jonas continued his advice, "This ranting and carrying on about John Singer and his supposed hidden identity will only cause undue harm, not only to John and Emma and the baby, but to you as well."

"How so?"

"As you know, very soon now the Booth conspirators will be found guilty of collusion with the assassin. They will be hung in Washington DC, possibly in early July."

"I did not know that."

"The government would not take kindly to your insinuations, of treason no less, in effect questioning their actions at Garrett's Barn this past April."

"Perhaps you are right."

"Henry," he sighed, looking tired. "Regardless of how suspicious John Singer acts, what he does or does not do is no concern of yours. I warned him to stay away from you and so I will say the exact same thing to you. The war is over. I need my talented surgeon back at the hospital in Alexandria. There are still so many who cannot leave who need your medical attention."

"Yes," Henry vaguely recalled, "I know of those poor soldiers and what they endured, their sacrifices. I know I must get well and take my place in Alexandria."

"Good," Jonas nodded, and looked relieved by the proper answers. "I will be leaving soon, returning to the hospital. Old Sam will stay here with you, as I cannot convince him otherwise. He is a loyal and devoted friend. Henry, he alone found you bleeding and unconscious in the stable. The sight broke his heart. He helped me care for you, to bring you back to health."

"I will be eternally grateful."

"Let us all help you now. Your parents are worried and very kind people. I was honored to meet them. They are waiting just outside the door, anxious to see their only child."

That thought made Henry's stomach clench. Deceiving Jonas about his true intentions was one thing, but facing his family would require true concentration and attention to every word.

"You are fortunate to be alive and you must stop all of this now in order to get well, but you must let go. Will you at least try?"

Henry reached, touching the hand of the worried Doctor Hendrix. As he feigned reassurance, he thought to himself, *"So now let the deception begin. Dear Jonas, not just to you, but to everyone."*

He then said in a meek and contrite voice, "Jonas, I am truly sorry for everything that has occurred. It all seems like a terrible dream, but in truth, I actually did all of these horrible things. I can't believe it! I am so humbly sorry."

Doctor Hendrix was listening.

"It started the day John Singer came into the hospital; he seemed just another patient, another in the thousand we treated. But there was something about him, almost familiar, haunting and challenging in his demeanor and ways."

He waited as he spun his tale, watched as Doctor Hendrix nodded to agree John Singer was not just another injured soldier at the Alexandria hospital.

"It wasn't until after our dear friend, Walt Whitman, mentioned to me how much this John Singer resembled Booth, I questioned it. I thought it perhaps because Walt was a friend to President Lincoln and was deeply saddened by his untimely death. Still, even in his grief, he seemed almost convinced of this notion with no proof other than how close the resemblance was and how vague Singer was about himself, never offering any family information or even tales of a battlefield fight."

"I will admit, that is odd," Jonas agreed.

"Yes, stories were all we heard from these soldiers in the four long years we worked, what battle they were in, their comrades and their memories about their dear loved ones at home. Things never once uttered by John Singer. It was a strange behavior, causing me to investigate a bit deeper. This became magnified when I realized that Emma was in love with John."

"It seems her affections for him were quite sudden and unexpected, something unforeseen."

"Yes, it was a shock to me. You see," he continued, "I just thought after the war I would tell Emma my feelings and that we would be married in the front parlor of her parents' house, like I had always dreamed of."

Henry hung his head. The strain of the deception gnawed at his heart as he drew another deep breath.

"Of course, I was wrong." He confessed words he hated to say, "Emma had no intentions of me, not as a husband and father to her children, but as a neighbor and friend."

Jonas could not believe his ears, hearing the calm and repentant Henry continue his soliloquy. It appeared the horrific murderous intentions and hateful rage that had consumed him was gone as quickly as it had reared its wrath, replaced now with the good man and doctor he respected.

He eyed his talented surgeon and carefully asked, "I am most pleased you have seen the error in your grievous ways, but such a drastic change of heart? You just had a conflict with Singer as we left the Dixon house, how is this possible?"

It was at those words that Henry knew Jonas was suspicious. The only way to deceive him, to convince his feigned change of heart was to appear repentant and humbled for his errant behavior these last few weeks.

He could do it.

He could convince everyone he was indeed sorry, make them believe that he only sought to make amends for that entire episode, the pain he had wrought.

But in truth, when the time is right, he intended to strike at the evil that was still alive and breathing in the Dixon House.

"Yes, I know," he softly said, trying to look remorseful, "but I am truly repentant. You must believe me. I have truly had a change of heart. You must believe me!"

Jonas seemed relieved to hear Henry's apologies, but he was not necessarily convinced. His tirades and rantings at the hospital and the mere fact he had hunted down John to kill him were not things quickly forgotten.

"Well, it is a step in the right direction." Jonas said with a slight frown. "But I will write to Miss Alcott and ask her to come to Richmond. In the meantime, your parents are still waiting in the hallway. I can't even describe the shock on their worried faces as I came to this house with you half unconscious and injured, carried in by Old Sam."

Henry bowed his throbbing head and thought of his parents. His father Thomas was a fine physician and educator. His mother, Sarah, a devoted and wholly spiritual woman who was deeply dedicated to her husband and son. He remembered their love and care of him, so proud when he graduated from medical school and equally proud to serve as a surgeon the war.

Then his thoughts turned dark, realizing the pain he must have caused them.

To them, he was truly sorry.

"Jonas," he whispered, "Please have my parents come in, and thank you for all you have done."

"I will return, remember that Henry." It was stated in a threatening tone, proving Jonas would be keeping an eye on him. "I hope to find you recovered and in a healthy state of mind. You must stay away from the Dixon House, entirely. Please keep in mind all I have said. You have been given a gift, don't waste it."

He turned away, opening the door to give entry to Henry's parents.

Henry sat up further against the pillow, as the sight of his family came into view. His father seemed so much older since the war ended, his hair having turned completely gray. His myopic blue eyes stare, the expression latent and heavy. He was thinner than before.

His mother Sarah was also thinner and grayer, with such pain in her eyes. Oh, the heartache he had caused. Too lost in his own heart and head, he never even considered how this would make the people he loved feel.

His father came to the bed and leaned down, embraced his son. To his surprise, the man cried. The sobs emitting from his father were heartbreaking to Henry's ears.

"I am so sorry for the pain I have caused you and mother. I truly am. Please forgive me."

Thomas stepped back, looked into the eyes that mirrored his own. "Doctor Hendrix explained all that has befallen you. I still cannot fathom any of it. Even worse is knowing you tried to take your own life."

"I'm sorry, Father."

"Henry, all those soldiers who you wrote to me about, the ones with missing arms, and legs and the men who cried out to you for help, I'm sure that took a toll on you."

"I could not work fast enough to save them."

His father seemed to truly understand a physician's heartache and pain. "I cried for you, and all those soldiers. But, to be in such an addled state you would attempt to take your own life? In your mistaken attempt to harm Emma's husband, John, she was accidently hurt. I can't believe you thought in that moment that taking your own life, with the understanding you had taken hers, was an option! Henry, death is never an option we choose. It comes for all of us at some point."

"Yes, I know you are right. Please, I am so sorry."

Those quiet words seemed to appease him. "You must rest, son, and start afresh. The war is over. We must move on with what the heavens gives us. Your mother and I are fortunate here in Richmond, we still have a roof over our heads, which is more than some of our friends. So you will recover now, here in the home you grew up in and forget all that happened."

"Thank you."

"Let it go." His father advised, "For if you continue to accuse Emma's husband, your words could bring the government upon us, and the swift hand of judgement. Is that what you want?"

Henry heard those words and truly did feel remorse.

"No, it is not what I want. I will try. I promise to stay away from the Dixon House. I am so very sorry for all that I have wrought, and you are correct, my most grievous mistake was thinking to take my own life. I never meant to cause you and mother hardship or pain. I will be well now, go on to be the son you are proud of."

His father drew a deep breath and looked relieved.

His mother Sarah then stepped forward, the tears falling from her eyes leaving small water drops upon the collar of her dress.

"Henry," she whispered, the sorrow in her eyes also trembling in her voice, "We can forgive you and it seems Mrs. Dixon has forgiven you. We are more fortunate than most for we are all together. So many families are lamenting the loss of a loved one. Please, do not add this family to that list. Please tell us now you will not attempt to take your life again, please."

Henry swallowed hard, the words to his parents sticking in his throat, but managed to murmur, "I promise Mother, I promise."

Sarah smiled then at her son, and said gently, "You must rest now. Old Sam is here. We will now consider him part of our family for the kindness, care and friendship he has shown you."

"Thank you. He is indeed a true friend."

Then both parents left his room, leaving Henry with only the solace of his racing thoughts to keep him company. Feeling stronger than he had in days, he needed to move. His body needed to gain more strength.

Henry slowly rose from his bed, wanting to go towards the windows that flooded his room with warm sunlight. His aching head caused a sense of vertigo, a slight dizziness. He walked gingerly, carefully navigating each step as to steady himself. Moving brought memories as his thoughts clouded with the sound of the derringer, the blood, the Dixon house, and the self-inflicted pain in his head.

He then came to the glass, exposed now without coverings or treatment and wondered about the rest of the house. He stood at the windows and blinked, as if trying to dispel the image that assaulted his sight.

He remembered his father's words. They were lucky to have a roof over their heads.

Looking out, he viewed neighboring homes in various states of destruction. Some burned and destroyed, with just the chimney stacks as a reminder of what once stood there.

Henry stared at Richmond until he thought he heard a sound behind him, as if someone was whispering his name. Confusion raced through his mind as he turned towards the sound.

Much to his astonishment, there stood Emma, resplendent in the gown she wore the night of her coming out party. She was like an angel, for it looked as if she was standing just inches above the floor.

No, not an angel.

She was a queen looking over her kingdom, her glossy pale hair hanging loose to her waist, strands of pearls woven like a crown into her tresses, her blue eyes shining.

They were focused on Henry.

Overwrought with disbelief, he could barely whisper, "Emma, is it really you? Oh, how beautiful you are. You came to me?"

The vision of pure womanly beauty smiled. To his ears her voice was like a cooing dove, "Why, of course I am here. I could not stay away from the only man I have ever loved. I am waiting for you. You must know, it is you I truly love, not John."

He was speechless.

"All those years at the hospital in Alexandria," she continued, "I waited for you to come to me. Yet, you never did. I believed we would never be together and so now I am married to John."

He felt so foolish for waiting to speak his heart to her.

"The child within me should be our child, Henry, not his."

Those words were like fire inside his heart.

"You must help me to be free from him. Marriage was a mistake. You will help me, won't you?" Emma stood motionless then, almost appearing to be locked in time as his mind raced over everything.

"Oh Emma," he blinked, his thoughts only of her, "all this time we have wasted. I adore you. I always have. I always will. You are my queen."

She seemed to return his affections, gave him a small smile. "You must find a way, Henry. You must come help me. I need you."

Henry stepped forward to be closer to his beloved.

"I have waited for you, my most precious Emma, waited to hear that you love me. Oh, how I love you." Needing to feel her touch he reached out. But to his dismay, as he did so, she began to fade from his view.

"No Emma, don't leave me."

Emma smiled a little brighter but continued to fade, like a figment of his imagination. "I must go now, but you only need to think of me, and I will return. You must come for me, Henry. Come and take me away from John. Only then can we be together."

He went to say something more but watched in astonishment as she faded from the room. Then he was alone. Henry shook his head feeling disoriented and lost. He suddenly realized he had not left his stance by the windows.

His eyes still looked outside at the burned destruction remaining of Richmond, a city forever ruined.

But it was real.

Emma had come to him, asked for his help.

He knew it deep inside.

"She loves me," muttered Henry, "She loves me! I only need to think of her and she will come to me." He smiled at this knowledge and walked slowly back to his bed, touching the sheets and pillows with his hands as if he were feeling them for the first time.

He kept saying over and over to himself, "She loves me, she loves me, she is mine." He thought of her husband and the ire rose up again within him. "He must be eliminated completely," he spluttered as he lay back against the pillows, his body feeling weighted by bricks. "But how?" He thought for a long time, staring at the ceiling.

Beau Jackson.

The name came as if someone spoke it.

"Ah, yes. Later I will ask Old Sam about exactly where in North Carolina the good Sergeant Jackson resides. I am sure Beau would want to know all that occurred since his release from the hospital. He will help get that diary. He will help me kill John Singer." A smile curved his lips as Henry finally gave into the blackness of sleep.

CHAPTER TEN

The Dixon Residence at Richmond, Virginia

"Emma, my darlin' we must go to Tudor Hall"
~~ John Wilkes Booth

John ran up the great marble steps, taking them two at a time missing the sight of his dear wife, Emma. The words of Doctor Hendrix still rang in his ears. He had to see Emma.

Every time they were parted he feared it may be the last time to see each other. John entered their bedroom to find beautiful Emma resting up against the bed frame, several pillows propped up behind her; the wounded shoulder was wrapped tight to aid in the healing. She wore only a white night gown. The day being warm enough she had pushed aside the heavy blankets.

John sat on the edge of the bed, taking his wife's hand, "My darlin' Emma, how is it possible I can miss you so much in such the shortest of time? For each time I think of you I cannot believe you are mine, the child is ours, and I am bound to you by something far grander than love." He kissed her forehead, feeling the heated sensation of desire within him. She was of such beauty and perfection, he wondered when the bloom of a child would begin within her and slowly sunk to his knees resting his head gently upon her still flat stomach and buried his face in her womanhood.

"Emma," he whispered, "I will wait, dearest wife until such time as the Doctor says you are well. At such time I shall take you dearest over and over again until you tell me no more. For it is as I said, you quench my thirst, yet I know after having you I am soon to be thirsty again. You are like an opiate. I cannot get enough."

Emma stroked his thick black hair. "My darling John, I feel the same way, even in this temporary condition where we must use restraint. I too am waiting for when I am well. And then John, I would ask you to take me over and over. For yes, we are bound by something far grander than love. I too am drawn to you by something stronger than love; just by being near to you sets my heart aflame."

John slowly kissed her through the gown, moving up her stomach and to her breasts, kissing and caressing. Finally moving his hand to her cheek, laying a gentle kiss upon her lips. Emma was breathless under his touch. As he moved from away she grasped his hand and once again placed it upon her breast. John smiled slyly as he whispered, "Soon my darlin' soon."

The seductive atmosphere of the room quickly dissipated as John's voice suddenly became serious. "I sent the telegraph to Asia. I told her I would bring you to Tudor Hall, for we must make plans. We cannot stay here in Richmond it's too dangerous."

"Henry is back at his parents' house by now; I saw him leaving with Old Sam, he was carrying Henry into your carriage with Doctor Hendrix. He did this to you, Emma, he shot you and tried to kill me, yet we cannot do anything to him. We can't go to the governing justice here in Richmond for fear of too much exposure. His addled brain is in such a state that his ranting poses a great danger to us."

"Yes, he is dangerous."

"I couldn't help it," John reluctantly confessed, "I told him about our baby. He saw me in the foyer and started his ranting again saying he was going to kill me."

"No John, no!"

"Then Doctor Hendrix came into the foyer and saw Henry's agitation. And Emma he said to me he didn't know who I was or what I trying to hide, but to stay away from Henry. He called me Singer, and then added, 'or should I call you Booth,' which was clearly a threat."

"He doesn't believe this, does he?"

John shook his head, "I do not know. But we cannot run that risk." As soon as we can, we will go to Tudor Hall. I hope, if all goes well, you will meet my family and my mother."

"What will you say to her? It will be quite a shock."

"My God, you are right," he suddenly realized how it might be. "My poor mother, what have I done to her? The fact that she thinks I am dead probably broke her heart, but what will happen when she sees me alive? Will she forgive me?" John hung his head as Emma reached and stroked his cheek. "My love, I believe once she sees you and holds you, she will love you as before. Ease your mind now, with such thoughts."

"This is not what I wanted for you Emma or our child. A life on the run, always fearful of the sudden knock on the door or the distant sound of approaching horses."

"Oh John," sighed Emma, "We must believe that Asia and your family will help us to stay safe. We must trust and believe in that. For we have no one else. I cannot tell Mother of who you really are, I cannot do that to her or to Abby."

"I understand."

"She bears so much with a heavy heart at the loss of dear father and my brother Caleb. She cannot think she will lose me and her grandchild as well. She must never ever know." She declared with determination. "It is for the protection of my family that at all cost, you are forever known as John Singer."

John's heart sank at the thought of what he had brought to Emma and the baby, "If we leave, we may never be able to return. What of the time when you are bearing the child? Do you not want your mother there to help you?"

"Our child has many more months to grow yet." She assured, "When the time comes, I will be strong for our child, for myself, and for my beloved husband."

John leaned over to Emma and placed a gentle wanting kiss on her desirous lips. "Is there anything you need right now, perhaps time to rest?"

"Not more rest. Although my shoulder is sore, I am in not in any pain. I would so love to get up from this bed and walk a bit, to feel the floor under my feet. Please?"

Emma looked at John, her blue eyes like perfect gems pleading at him. He could deny her nothing. He gently brought her upright, helped her stand.

She smiled, looking triumphant, even in her nightgown. "Now, help me get dressed. I've been in that bed for long enough. Let us walk a bit just down the hallway and back please?"

He brought her clothes. As he helped her change, he mused about her ability to persuade him. "Ah tell me darlin', what spell have you cast upon me that I am unable and unwilling to deny you anything?"

"John," she turned in his arms and kissed him, "It is the spell of love that has you bound and tied to me forever."

"I am your most willing captive."

Emma looked at John, a lazy smile upon her lips. "You are profoundly handsome, dear husband, a fact so true as I look upon your face. And so I ask, who has captured whom?"

Both husband and wife laughed the intimacy and bond of such a deep love that would test them as they moved forward in their married lives, unsure of the path that it would take them.

◆

Annabelle heard laughter in the upstairs hallway from her bedroom as she went to check on Abby. She came out from her room anxious to see about the commotion and not to disturb the child who was still sound asleep. The concerned mother followed the torn Persian hallway carpet runner from her door until she found both John helping Emma, walking ever so gingerly and laughing intimately under the security of married love.

"Emma, what are you doing?" cried Mrs. Dixon. "John, no, please take my daughter back to bed. She must rest."

"Mother," cajoled Emma, "Please, it is I who asked John to take me to walk. I just wanted to stretch and feel my legs work again."

She shook her head in disbelief, "Come back to your room and rest, you must think of the child and your strength."

Emma stood her ground and said stubbornly "I promise I will have John take me back shortly. I just need to walk for just a while longer."

"Very well. I tell you what, why don't I go into your room and tidy up a bit? Then when you return, I will have fresh linens for you it will make you more comfortable. Then will you rest?"

"Yes. Thank you."

The whole time standing in the hallway John said nothing. Annabelle took stock of her handsome son-in-law, truly an extraordinary looking man. His dark glossy hair fell about his noble face. His eyes were equally black, so much so that it seemed there was no iris, only an inky compelling darkness. They were stunning and riveting all at once. His white marble skin was lightly tanned now from days in the sun, only adding to the beauty of this man.

Their child together would be magnificent.

"Very well. I will see to your room right now. Annabelle turned down the hallway to the newly married couple's room. She set about to tidy the room as quickly as possible. She went over to the old armoire the one that recently housed Emma's wedding gown.

Annabelle had salvaged some linen from various places in the house. Never minding that the linens were patched from whatever was left in the house when she returned after the war.

She lingered over a patch of French blue bed linens from when Emma left for Alexandria now torn and shredded, a sad reminder of what was and would never come again. No sense lamenting, not today when the daughter that could have died could now be heard laughing as she walked the upper halls.

She then hastened her step as she went about her business. She reached into the open armoire and hastily grabbed the linen pile as she did she noticed a small red book that fell at her feet. It must have been stuck inside the linens.

Annabelle reached down at her feet. Picking it up, the pages opened unexpectedly. Out fell what looked like folded news articles, a letter not sent or received as it had no postmark and several other news pages. She looked at the scattered materials and noticed the name and address of the letter.

Asia Booth Clarke, Raceway, Philadelphia PA.

Not thinking more of it, she distantly remembered Emma had left for a short overnight visit to Philadelphia right after marrying John.

Annabelle remembered Emma had told her and John it was urgent business with a former nurse from the same Alexandria hospital who was gravely ill and was asking to see Emma.

But then something began to nag at her. Perhaps it was the name "Booth" on the envelope or the incredulous statement from Jonas on Henry's rantings that somehow her son in law was really John Wilkes Booth. Or, perhaps it was the mention from her kind neighbor Eleanor. Who, upon seeing John for just that fleeting moment said he reminded her of someone. Annabelle reached into the envelope and removing the letter. It was she was sure, nothing at all.

She scanned the letter as she read the greeting, *"My dearest sister Asia" and such words ..."hunted down with every man's hand against me" and...." please forgive me,"* and finally like a dagger through her heart she read, *"tell mother I died for my country,"* there was more but she placed the letter back into the envelope.

With hands shaking she unfolded the news articles about the hunt for the assassin of Abraham Lincoln, John Wilkes Booth, and his named conspirators.

And then finally to the other folded news like articles which as with each unfold felt like agony as the truth was finally revealed to her. The handsome face on the WANTED poster was familiar now. She noted various diary entries written with the same cursive script as the letter and closed her eyes.

Annabelle sunk to her knees in disbelief as she agonized to herself, "My God, Emma. You have married a murderer."

She looked at it all again, the truth clear.

"It cannot be. It just cannot be true. Your husband is John Wilkes Booth, and my grandchild is a Booth, a name that is stained with murder. Oh my daughter, you are in the gravest danger, as are all of us. We should have believed Henry."

Annabelle remained on her knees as she rocked back and forth in disbelief. "Emma," she whispered, feeling she barely knew her daughter anymore. "Who was the woman that came back with you from Philadelphia; I had heard of a beautiful visitor that came back with you while Abby and I were out looking to call on neighbors and offer what we could to help them."

"I did not think much of this as she did not stay long nor did you say anything much about her visit."

Annabelle gasped out loud as it occurred to her then, "There was no such ill nurse that was calling for you!"

"It was John's sister! It had to have been his sister you found this letter too, and found your way to Philadelphia to convince his sister he was alive! How brave yet foolish to commit such an act," she thought, "Yet how was it that John would have not gone himself to contact his sister?"

She puzzled over this and finally realized Emma probably never told him she knew his true identity. Perhaps she learned who he was as innocent as she just had. She knew and married him anyway. Annabelle recalled the conversation that Emma was expecting and had admitted being with John before their marriage.

She drew in a deep breath, thinking of her handsome son-in-law and the feigned persona of a dead Confederate soldier John Singer. Rising to her feet, she carefully put the diary back into the armoire, hoping her removal of the linens would not reveal the diary's former resting place. She felt sick and dizzy as she realized her daughter and grandchild's future and the grave danger that would follow her on her life in deception and on the run.

She realized Henry was right about believing Singer was Booth, but she would not seek to find out. He posed a danger to Emma. He was back at his family's home recovering. She had already told Jonas she would not pursue any judicial investigation into the shooting. Now, she was grateful for her generous decision as any inquiry could have brought more questions to Henry and his beliefs. It would have brought a possible investigation on John Singer.

Annabelle then made her way to the bed to refresh it. She hurried now, as both John and Emma would be returning soon. She removed the linens and replaced them with fresh ones, all the while trying to dispel all that that had been revealed to her.

It did no good.

She knew the truth now. But she vowed not to tell Emma or anyone she knew of the ruse. She would, however, do anything, at all costs to see her Emma and grandchild to safety. If her daughter chose to believe in John's good heart, she would trust that. She would carry on. The knowledge did nothing but harm. Emma was Mrs. John Singer. She was not and would ever be known as Mrs. John Wilkes Booth.

"God help me," she whispered, "That I may carry this out."

She was still murmuring this as John entered the room holding the hand of her beloved Emma. She looked up as he entered, his dark eyes shining and intent on Emma. Annabelle felt angry; she glared at him and bore her eyes to his. How dare he endanger the people she loved?

Emma noticed the glare in her mother's eyes, "Mother, are you all right? You look like you have seen a ghost!"

Annabelle drew in her breath deeply as she met Emma's query and replied evenly, "Yes child, I am just fine and to answer your question, no I haven't seen a ghost," but mumbled to herself, "Just perhaps the devil himself."

John heard this and arched a brow, unwilling and unable to say anything more.

CHAPTER ELEVEN

The Bradley Residence in Richmond, Virginia

"Dear Sergeant Jackson..."
~~ Henry Bradley

Henry awoke from a deep night of sleep, the sunlight of a new day once again flooding his room through the uncovered windows. He closed his eyes again and remembered with euphoria Emma coming to him and confessing she loved him. Soon they would be together forever, just like they were supposed to be. He would find a way.

He noticed his faithful friend Old Sam resting on a pallet on the floor and realized his every move would be watched. As he stirred and sat up, Old Sam heard the movements and roused himself, his big frame taking a moment to rise from the floor before coming to sit in the chair beside the bed.

"Doc Hendrix, he done left back to Alexandria." He informed, as was his habit of always keeping Henry abreast of any news. "But he said youse gonna be okay. Youse just needed some rest, and some eatin' too. I almost lost you, friend. I thought you was a gonner, for sure." Old Sam shook his head and looked terribly sad before meeting his gaze again with watery eyes, "But youse alive Doc, and I'm here to see you stay alive and be well."

"Thank you, Sam."

"I've been powerful worried about you," the large black man confessed, "chasing after Mister John."

Henry thought for a moment, the workings of his mind seeming to take longer than normal, his mind churning slowly as he realized he must also convince Old Sam of his repentance for his ravings and behavior.

It was the only way to see his plan to fruition.

For truly in the end, Emma would thank him for ridding her of the weight of marriage to that man.

After all, she asked for his help.

"I am sorry for everything." He gently told Old Sam, keeping his eyes looking at his hands in his lap. "I have been exhausted and so full of anguish for those we tended and lost at the hospital. I still can hear their cries old friend, cries that I could do nothing about as they died all around me."

Old Sam seemed to consider those terrible anguished days serving at the Alexandria field hospital during the war. Many times they worked some twenty hours straight trying to save lives; yet, it was never enough as the wounded and dying kept coming. He had witnessed the blood seeping everywhere such that a mop or rags were no match to keep up. They both had days when the blood stained their shoes clear through, yet, they had carried on.

"Yes suh," reminisced Old Sam. "I sure done remember those terrible days, and all them boys and men sufferin' and screamin' and I done saw your face every time one of them poor souls passed away."

His own head bowed, his expression tormented by the overwhelming loss they had both endured.

"What is it?"

"I saw your sufferin' too," the big man confessed, "but you done the best you could. We all did. But, I just didn't understand all that stuff about Miss Emma."

Henry had no words.

Old Sam continued, "I was happy she found herself a man to love. She done suffered too, losing her pappy and brother in the battle. And you told me you knew the Dixon family, them bein' friends with your Ma and Pa."

"Yes, I have known them all my life."

"But now you is home with your own family, with those who love you and only want you to get well."

Everything Sam said was true.

Emma did deserve a man to love.

But not that imposter. He was the better man and he would prove it. Henry looked into eyes of his dear friend, "I am inherently sorry for the pain I caused and the crimes I commitment in coming after John and Emma."

He had Sam's undivided attention.

"I had truly hoped she would find favor with me." Henry looked toward the window, recalling seeing Emma last night. Another secret, for his heart only.

"But alas," he sighed in resignation, "it was not meant to be. Her heart belongs to another. She is married to him and they are expecting a child." He tried to add a lilt of happiness for the couple's news to his voice. "There will be no more talk of vengeance to John Singer, no more."

The old hospital attendant was not so easily convinced. Old Sam looked at him with stern eyes and a slight frown. Having been around to witness Doctor Bradley's rants and exhaustive banter, and of course the ultimate act of actually chasing after John and Miss Emma, he was not so gullible as to believe this sudden change of heart.

"But Doc you just saw Mister John at the Dixon house, and you sounded angrier and angrier, especially after he done told you about that baby. I'm worried about you. I ain't so book smart, but I do know somptin about people." His thick arms folded over his broad chest, "You will have a lot more convincing to do to make me believe you is a changed man."

This would be much more difficult than Henry anticipated. Old Sam may be simple, but he was not dumb.

"It is true, I have let you down, and yes Doctor Hendrix too, who risked much with you to come and find me, trying to save me from myself. I can only from this time forward prove to be repentant of my terrible deeds and perhaps to show John and Emma I am truly sorry by apologizing to them face to face."

"Youse ain't going nowhere near them."

"But it wasn't me, Old Sam, it was as if something hateful had taken hold of me. That thing raged and raged until I became that horrible manifestation of a most grievous creature." Henry let his voice catch, showing a struggle with emotions. "You know me my friend, you know me. We worked together trying to save our soldiers. We saw some terrible things, but the one thing I do know is that we stuck together and helped each other through years of such horrible sights."

"It's true. The war was awful bloody."

"So now you see, I have been through such a spell, but I'm coming out of it now. I'm trying. I can only reach out and ask you as my only and dearest friend to help me through his time now a time of repentance. Please, am I at least to be forgiven?"

Henry held out his hand in solidarity to his old and devoted friend. Old Sam shook his hand. "Youse tellin' me, you is honestly repentant and sorry?" Henry nodded. "But, just for my sake, I will be keeping a close eye on you, just in case"

His large hand released Henry's as he stood, towering over the bed without intending to be intimidating, he was just that big. From the bed where he reclined against the pillows, Henry had to look up at him.

"I'm gonna be right with you." Old Sam declared. "Always. Just in case the sight of Mister John and Miss Emma gives you pause, brings you any ideas to wrangle up trouble for them once again. And so you are given a second chance, but with the eyes of one who knows you, through and through."

Henry smiled, showing his gratitude. "That is all I could reasonably ask for right now. I am in no position to ask for more."

Strolling about the bedroom in an aimless manner that was familiar to the big man's ways, Old Sam felt chatty now, sharing gossip like he always had.

"Well, I done heard that Doc Hendrix is heading up to Alexandria back to the hospital." He offered the knowledge, "Says he aims to be fixing a new head Doctor there just fer a spell. Then he's coming back up here to check on you and Miss Emma, and so I as heard too, to pay a call on Mrs. Dixon!"

As Henry heard this last remark he wrinkled his eyebrows, and queried, "Sam did you just say Doctor Hendrix intended to pay a call, a social call on Mrs. Dixon. Really? How is that possible? You must have it wrong."

Old Sam stood his ground in the explanation of the truth as he knew it. "No Doc I is not wrong. I seen the look in them two's eyes each time they met."

"Oh, really?"

"I saw it when I went to find Mrs. Dixon to fetch you a clean linen by orders of Doctor Hendrix, cause you was hurt. Her expression was so sad as she handed over what looked like some fancy table work, handed it over with grace and ease, as if every day she gave over her prized linens to be used as hospital rags."

Henry considered those words.

"There was somptin about her face. See then, finally after tendin' you and Miss Emma, Doctor Hendrix finally paid a proper call to the mistress and of course even in her distress was gracious and kind to those who helped save you and Emma. She asked him to please stay a spell to eat, as a thank you for his kind service. I didn't hear more, 'cept that he was a comin' back as soon as he could, and not just for the patients that needed tending."

It was interesting news.

"Seems to me they have found favor with one another." Henry mused, deciding Sam must be right. "Imagine in the deepest part of sorrow and fear the good fortune of finding a kind heart. In the midst of such pain, it is truly a gift."

"Much like how Miss Emma done found favor with Mister John. Sometimes the heart has other plans."

"Ah Sam" said Henry, "Sometimes is wise you are."

He feigned a smile as he realized as tired as he was, there was a task he wanted to ask of old Sam. The budding romance of Jonas and Mrs. Dixon would have little if anything to do with his plan of revenge. He scoffed at that fact and took a deep breath as he thought of how to present exactly what he needed from Old Sam in order to get his plan in motion.

But carefully.

Or the watchful man would see right through it.

"Say Old Sam," eased Henry, "I was wondering if you could locate some writing paper for me? I would sure like to write to a soldier friend of mine, you remember him right, the fellow that in the infirmary next to Mister John, you remember the one that was in the Battle of the Wilderness?"

Old Sam knotted his eyebrows in an effort to remember one of the thousands that crossed his path those four long years. Then suddenly he cried out, "Why yes suh, I sure do remember him, let's see I think his name was Billy or Beau or something like that. Yes suh, he done suffer something fierce, told me about them fellers burning alive in that fire, the ones too injured to escape out. Ah yes that one I remembered."

"Lucky it was just his arm that got blown off." Henry recounted.

"You done seen him off, if I recollect right," the big man continued. "You know, he is from the same town, in North Carolina as me. But I believe he was from good people. I think he said he was fighting the war just to protect his small farm and his way of life."

Henry agreed, "Yes, he was a farmer."

"He never did have slaves." Sam firmly seemed to approve of Beau Jackson. "So what fer you wanting to write to him?"

"Well Sam," began Henry, "I guess with time on my hands now with nothing to do except rest and heal, I thought to reach out to a few of the former patients, just see how they are getting along."

Satisfied with the ease of Henry's lie, Old Sam went to find the paper and quill for his friend, only too happy to oblige the task asked of him.

Henry leaned back on the pillows, his head once again aching but he would not rest until he had that paper and quill, and to think of the words that would bring Beau to Richmond.

He drew in his breath as he waited for Old Sam to appear, and much to his gratitude a tray appeared with writing paper and envelopes and a quill and ink. He leveled his glee at such a sight, not willing to divulge to Sam the excitement he felt building within him, excitement as to the words he would write to Sergeant Jackson, the remembering the words he told him those months ago as he slipped the derringer in Henry's hands, "Some people just need killin."

"That's right there, Beau they sure do, and only this time I'll have help." He smiled with that thought and was still smiling as Old Sam handed him the tray and moved to sit on the makeshift couch to keep watch over his friend.

❖

Dear Sergeant Jackson:

*I hope this finds you well, your wife and little girl the
same. And of course, I send good thoughts that your farm
was spared when the burning of the Atlanta commenced, and
then to the Carolinas in the path of General Sherman's Union
forces. I can only hope you and your family were spared such
loss and misery.*

*I write to you as a favor is requested. I am here in
Richmond, VA at my parents' home, resting or so they think,
healing that which affects my aching heart.*

*You see, I remember your parting words to me at the
hospital in Alexandria, when you slipped the derringer in my
hand and told me "some people just need killin."*

*Ah how perceptive you were friend, very much so. That
former hospital mate of yours, John Singer, is most definitely
a fraud, a fake and a murderer.*

*By some evidence I know exists and by his ghostly cryptic
actions, I know this man is in hiding. He claims not to recall
his past because the truth of the matter is that he was never in
the war, never fought like you and your brethren. But rather
than offering true courage and sacrifice, the man feigned
glory by play acting upon the stage and was revered for his
acting bravely. He was playacting while the rest of mankind
sacrificed themselves.*

*Singer is not shell shocked, nor is he addled in any sense of
the word. He is cunning and will get away with murder,
unless we stop him.*

*For that mysterious soldier John Singer is no soldier at all,
but rather a murderer, the murderer who killed our President
Abraham Lincoln.*

John Singer is John Wilkes Booth.

The evidence adds up.

*He came into the hospital at the very end of the war, his
left leg broken, in a temporary cast. Reports from those
present at Ford's Theatre saw Booth break that leg in his
effort to get away.*

*Booth should have died in that barn fire that night when
they caught up to him, but instead he escaped and now lives
in hiding under some feigned name.*

*Remember Old Sam? He is here with me at the behest of
Doctor Hendrix to watch me. Why, you ask do I need tending?*

You see, in the days after you left Alexandria, the derringer you gave me weighted comfortingly inside my pocket, a comfort only you would understand.

But comfort it did, indeed, for now I had the means to hunt that traitor down and kill him. It would be a double pleasure to do this deed, for the rightful killing of Booth and for freeing Emma from that madman's spell.

Yes, I had many reasons to want him dead, but providence was not on my side when I caught up to him in the Dixon's stable in Richmond. I aimed at John, but Emma lunged to protect her husband. I thought I had killed her, but later learned it was a shoulder wound.

In my delirium, believing I murdered my precious Emma, in that moment I felt my life was over.

I reloaded the gun, raising it again, not at John but at myself. If Emma were dead, I needed to join her. But my hand shook and the bullet grazed my temple.

Now I am recovering from a self-inflicted gunshot wound while Emma heals at the Dixon home, her husband John by her side.

And yes, there is news of a child, as well.

My beautiful Emma is expecting his child.

Beau, this is wrong.

You saw it then. You know it now. I ask all the powers of our friendship that was forged on the bondage of blood and death, that you come to Richmond forthwith. Please help me finish the task that is still undone.

Old Sam has seen the diary that John kept, which he claims has papers and news clipping, documents to support his true identity.

We must find that diary and take it to Washington, to prove that an imposter was killed at Garrett's Farm.

We will them watch as the hand of the government silences once and for all, the man known as John Singer. And then you and I will be lauded as the bravest of all men, for being the bringers of justice.

And then Emma shall be mine.

Think hard on this Beau, think hard.

But keep in your mind's eye the ones who died so horribly, like the ones you heard burning to death in the thick brush of the Battle of the Wilderness, screaming in agony. Do you think this imposter would ever have sacrificed so much, how they did?

Never.

No one knows of this plan.

All those here in Richmond are still weighing my change of heart, from being an addled killer to becoming a quiet man of gentle repentance.

Only you know the truth. In this way I keep my deception complete as I carefully calculate and consider Singer's next move. Steady my friend, your time to help in our retribution is near.

Write me soon and please come to Richmond.

Henry Bradley, MD

CHAPTER TWELVE

The Dixon Residence in Richmond, Virginia

"I know who you really are."
~~ Annabelle Dixon

John stood silent as he watched his mother-in-law help Emma back into bed and smooth back the fresh linens, fluffing the pillow for her daughter to rest more comfortably. As she turned, her eyes bore into him, her stare intense and direct.

"John" asked Annabelle, "Perhaps you and I can sit a spell and have a visit in the parlor while Emma gets her rest. I think we have much to discuss, so much has happened I can barely understand any of it. You will help me try to understand, won't you?" She smiled at him then as her practiced southern charm and melodious voice warmed the room.

John bowed slightly in deference to his mother-in-law his manners polished and smooth, his demeanor equal to her southern charm.

It was only after the large cherry doors in the parlor had been closed and only after Mrs. Dixon gestured for her son in law to sit that she began to speak.

"John you are now a part of my family, a family that includes myself, Emma and the baby and of course Abigail," Mrs. Dixon began her voice steady and controlled.

"Like most families of the south especially here in Richmond we have lost loved ones to the war. You must know how very dearly I love Emma."

"It has been almost unbelievable to think that our Emma was shot by our family's dearest neighbor, Doctor Henry Bradley. I cannot fathom that and to know now that that bullet was meant for you John isn't that right?"

"Yes, it was."

Not waiting for an answer she continued, "I have wracked my mind trying to understand what could have happened to our Henry that as a Doctor who worked tirelessly for four years to save our sons of the south and now at the end of the war he could turn into a killer."

"You know Mr. Dixon had hoped the Bradley family and the Dixon family would be well, how should I say, be more than just neighbors, but now that is not what happened exactly now did it? My Emma followed her heart and heart led itself right to you. Again without waiting for an answer she continued on, "You are quite the gentleman John, and so very charming." Mrs. Dixon leaned into John as her lips formed a firm resolute line across her angry face, her eyes suddenly flashing and intent.

John suddenly rose from his sitting position and said pointedly, "Emma and I love each other. I don't deserve her or her love, but it was Emma's choice not to consider Doctor Bradley a proper suiter for her affection."

"A proper suiter you say!" She fumed, "Who are you to say who is a proper suitor or not!"

John stood silent unsure of how to answer and unsure of what was going on.

She turned away from John as her fury rose from her heart, then whirled again to face him.

"I know who you really are. You are a murderer!" She hissed the words. Her eyes were icy cold blue, as they looked into John's dark eyes. She said again, "You are a murderer, Mr. Booth. That is who you are. Yes, I know. You are John Wilkes Booth, the assassin!"

He did not know what to say.

Annabelle was on a roll, "Don't deny this John don't even try, Henry isn't addled with hysteria or exhaustion from the war, but rather with the knowledge that our dear sweet Emma is really married to a low count lying, murdering scoundrel. Here I have welcomed you like the son I lost, happy for my child and the child she is to bear, now knowing your true identity and hiding under the false name of John Singer."

She paced the floor, her thoughts being spat out without social niceties or a filter. "Emma should have let you die in that hospital instead of risking hers to save the likes of you. I have a mind to go over to the Bradley's and tell Henry he is right, and you are Booth." She whirled again, facing him once more. "And what do you think John? After all, he followed you and Emma here to Richmond to kill you, and expose the fraud that you are."

"What lead you to believe this?"

Mrs. Dixon continued, "I found the diary with the letter to Asia Booth Clarke and the entries that said, 'hunted down with every man's hand against me.' It fell out of from between the linens when I when to change them. Don't insult me by trying to deny it."

"I cannot."

His simple honest admittance stole all of her angry fire. Instantly, tears watered in her eyes. "You realize you have brought death to our home, by your mere existence?"

Annabelle now had tears streaming down her face.

"My God, my God," whispered John. "I am so very sorry. I cannot deny any of what you said, not one word of it. Yes, it is all true. And so I ask you, Annabelle, what is it you will have me to do?"

John bowed his head to his mother-in-law, his heart heavy and fearful, heavy because of his deception for he truly loved her, yet was fearful of what she would do.

Annabelle sighed deeply, "John, I cannot truly believe any of this is happening, I am stunned, and heart broken. I only know there is terrible, terrible danger here. My daughter and grandchild, what is to become of them? You have brought this terrible scourge to my house, to Emma's house to what would have been your house. I cannot speak anymore I am most bereft."

She seemed to wilt, sitting down in a chair.

"Annabelle," began John, "If I could change what I did I would, but those who cajoled me and told me I was the only one to remove the tyrant from the throne have abandoned me. I have no more to say of this. I can only now try to survive and keep my identity hidden."

She listened, sniffing occasionally.

"I have written to my sister Asia in Philadelphia. That is where I was going earlier today, to the telegraph office to tell her of the terrible events that happened here after she left and to tell my family we are in mortal danger here. I share this with you now. Please know that as soon as possible I will take Emma to my boyhood home in Maryland. There, with my family I will figure out what to do."

Annabelle looked at her son-in-law, her facial expression twisted in fear. "And then what John, then what? Where do you think you can hide and who will help Emma with the baby?"

"I cannot honestly answer that. I am hoping to find a little corner somewhere in his world to take Emma and our child. I will enlist the assistance of my brothers. At Tudor Hall, I will tell my siblings I am alive, married and in need of help."

Annabelle shook her head back and forth many times before she could speak. Her words came out slowly as if it took all her energy to respond. "I am bound now and part of this great conspiracy. Your presence here confirms that. There is nothing more I would want to do, then run and tell Henry he is right, to tell Emma I know everything, to shout it out to the world the killer not only lives, but is here in Richmond."

"I beg you, pray you do not."

She shook her head, "You know I will not. Shouting your name in the streets would bring a reign of terror to my door, to Emma and the baby. Your death will be her death and the death of that child. I will tell no one," she vowed, looking him in the eyes, "Not one mortal soul, not even my precious daughter will know I have discovered the truth."

John was speechless as the truth of his true identity came to light.

With steely anger in her voice she said to her son in law, "I do this for her sake, not yours. Remember that."

She then found her strength and stood again. She marched up and leaned in close, her face just inches from his. Her lovely drawl was sinister as she warned him, "If anything happens to Emma or the baby because of you, just know that while I shall never speak of this again, I will hunt you down like nothing you've ever experienced and I will kill you without a morsel of regret in my body. At that moment you will know that death by my hand will have been far worse than that burning barn at Garrett's farm."

With that said, Annabelle nodded her head in affirmation and strode out of the room, never looking back to see the stunned expression on John's face.

CHAPTER THIRTEEN

The Bradley Residence in Richmond, Virginia

"Dearest Henry I shall not abandon you"
~~ Louisa May Alcott

The hired carriage Walt and Louisa took from the train depot in Richmond was nothing more than an old buckboard with a makeshift slab of wood for the two passengers to sit upon. The wagon hitched and lurched along the deeply rutted and war-torn roads of Richmond.

And so then for several miles the two of them said nothing as the devastation of the once fine city spoke for itself in the masses of broken homes, businesses burned. The worst part of all was the deafening silence broken only by sounds as the buckboard squealed and pulled forward.

"Walt," said Louisa, "This is beyond anything I expected to see. I heard Richmond was burned, but this is beyond anything I could have imagined."

The old gent whose eyes seemed permanently rimmed in red from having seen so much loss, especially since mourning the death of President Lincoln, surveyed the scene.

"These last four years we endured the daily death and hearing the screams of pain from those poor soldiers at the hospital, but now we see the true devastation of the war." His gray head shook in sorrow and disbelief. "Richmond has suffered the cruelest blow. This was the Capital of the Confederacy. For this, the city paid an even higher price."

"Yes, it did. It's sad to see."

Again, they rode in silence.

Louisa finally asked, "What do you think we will find when we see Henry? I still don't understand what happened to such a fine physician. How could he try to murder someone?"

"Ah Miss Louisa," the poet mused, "I am no stranger to the stories of survival, death and even things that cannot be explained. Perhaps in our deepest longing and fears, God does hear us and sends us things that we cannot understand, but we must accept. Perhaps that is what God is asking of you and I now, to help the wounded soul of one who saved so many."

"Perhaps you are right."

"It is time now to stop, stop all of it," he let he wisdom of his private thoughts be heard.

"Yes, it is time."

"The war is over. It is time to live and rebuild." Walt added his philosophy on the state of the nation, "The country is as one now. And we must go on as one, together to help where we can and heal those broken hearts, bodies and spirits. It's the least we can do for the ones that survived."

"It's good then," she agreed, "We stop at Henry's first. Then perhaps tomorrow we will stop in on the Dixon's and check on Emma and her John, of course."

Walt sighed in thinking all that waited ahead of them, all that lay behind them.

"Miss Louisa, so much has happened in these past few weeks. Months, and years, too. Yet, look around you. The few trees left standing still show the glory of the dogwood blooms bringing forth such beauty in the midst of this desolation." He gazed in appreciation at the beautiful pink trees as they rode past. "It is a sign that Richmond will rebuilt to its former glory."

Louisa was not as optimistic and could only feign a smile as she looked at the few remaining dogwood trees that lined the streets. They must have once stood in solidarity around the great homes they had graced.

Gone now, so many of them. Burned to ashes.

The buckboard slowed it pace and finally came to stop in front of a formerly lavish two-story white home with two Doric columns on each side of the front securing up to the second-floor portico. A gilded gold leaf pattern twisted upon the top of each column.

Louisa sighed in disappointment to see large sections of the gold leaf had been ripped from the stone, a reminder of the desperation of the times.

They quickly surveyed the exterior of the house seeing further signs of the destruction from the war. Rubble still littered the street, and although the walkway to the Bradley residence had been swept clean, it too had been damaged by soldiers. The house still stood intact yet showing grievous signs of war.

This home, however, fared much better than several of its neighbors.

The Dixon's were fortunate.

The hired drayman assisted them out of the buckboard. Walt paid the fee. The driver bowed and climbed aboard again, and then turned the rented buckboard around to leave.

Louise and Walt carefully picked their steps to the front entrance the pavers that once held an opulent design now broken and littered the once grand entrance.

They walked to the front door, anxious to see Henry, and Walt turned the large brass bell. It echoed through what seemed to be many rooms, chiming through the emptiness of the large but spare house.

The door cautiously opened, only to be suddenly flung wide open upon realizing who waited outside. Louisa gasped as the sight of Old Sam stood there, his bulk filling up one side of the double French entrance.

"Miss Louisa," he grinned.

"Old Sam, you are here."

It was for those few first moments, surreal as a great joy was felt to see one another. Yet as quickly as the reunion of joy began it ended, as the pallor of the true reasons for Miss Louisa and Mr. Walt's visit was realized.

It was Louisa who stepped forward.

"Doctor Hendrix has told me all of what happened and asked us here to help. Is Henry well enough for visitors and may we see him?"

Old Sam looked down at the floor, his feet scuffing over the dusty marble flooring and said to his friends, "Well, he just now finished some writtin' that seemed to make him powerful happy, so he may be restin' a spell."

"Oh, is he terribly unwell?"

"His wound from his head is healing pretty good, but you know, it's the wound in his heart and mind still has us worried." Admitting so much seemed to trouble Old Sam. He swung the front door open wide.

"Come here into the parlor. You must be tired and powerful hungry after that long trip." He remembered his manners. "I'll go find the Lady of the house and tell her you are here."

"Thank you."

They followed him inside the home as Old Sam felt the need to explain the situation further. "Mrs. and Doc Bradley are lettin' me stay with Henry and have offered their home to me, fo' as long as we needs. They are kind people. They too have been sorely devastated by what Henry has done."

"It is regretful, indeed."

Both Louisa and Walt sat tentatively upon what remained of the parlor furniture. It was not burned or destroyed but it appeared the house had been looted during the war. What remained were just the bare walls and whatever broken pieces of furniture that were not worth taking.

They had no more time to linger as Mrs. Sarah Bradley entered the parlor with her husband Doctor Thomas Bradley, who seemed eager looking forward to meeting some of Henry's friends from the Alexandria hospital, and perhaps to try to understand what may have happened to their dear and suffering son.

Mrs. Bradley entered the room and greeted them, Henry's friends. She then reached for Miss Alcott and Mr. Whitman with a true and open heart.

Mrs. Bradley made an elegant yet easy motion with her hands, indicating them to sit upon the parlor furniture, a gesture learned from years of skilled etiquette.

"Both my husband Thomas and I are eternally grateful you have come to aid in Henry's recovery. Doctor Hendrix told us of your friendship and camaraderie. We thank you for your expediency in traveling to Richmond."

"Your welcome, Madam," Walt nodded.

"Please stay as long as you wish."

It was Louisa who spoke softly of their own feelings regarding the situation and friendship, "I owe a debt of service to your son. Henry assisted me through a very difficult time. There was never a question for both Walt and I to come. Your kind hospitality is only surpassed certainly by the love you have for your son. We are honored to be here."

With that said, Mrs. Bradley motioned to her guests at the girl who stood waiting, "Our house maid, Chloe, will see to your rooms."

"Thank you."

"Dinner will be at 8:00 and we shall reacquaint at that time. For now, please take your rest and feel free to visit with Henry after dinner."

Walt and Louisa followed the servant through the house. Their footsteps echoed throughout the empty foyer on the bare marble and up stone steps going to the upstairs rooms.

◆

Henry heard familiar voices outside his bedroom and listened but could not identify who he heard. Old Sam appeared, gingerly opening his door. "You doing okay there, Doc? Hope we didn't wake you."

"No, I am fine. I have finished my letter to Sergeant Beau Jackson." He had already sealed it with wax, ensuring his words would be for the recipient alone. He handed it over to Old Sam, entrusting his friend with this most important document. "Could you take it to the dispatch office?"

Old Sam liked being useful to Henry and being asked made him happy. He had a wide and toothy grin, "Well now, suh. I will most surely deliver it."

"Who did I hear out there?" asked Henry.

"It was none other than Miss Louisa and Mr. Walt. They just arrived."

Henry felt shocked at first, and then smiled inwardly. "They think I need care and watching?"

Sam nodded. "They worried 'bout you."

"Well, they will soon see I am doing fine."

"Yes, suh. They is getting' settled in, but will come and sit a spell with you, after a while."

"I look forward to it."

Holding the letter in his large fist, Sam closed the door, leaving Henry alone with his thoughts.

"I am a very different man from the one that left Alexandria a few weeks ago," thought Henry, looking out the sunny window. "They will bear witness to a very repentant man now, as I wait for Sergeant Beau to come to Richmond and help me finish the task of what I failed to do."

◆

As evening fell and the last waning rays of daylight gave over to dusk, Old Sam checked to see that Henry was up and that his dinner tray was now empty of the evening's fare. Satisfied he had eaten and was ready for visitors, Walt and Louisa came. They stood in the hallway waiting to cross the threshold to see Henry.

Henry saw concern on Walt's face and remembered the old gent at the hospital, his brilliant words given to the countless dying soldiers they tended.

Louisa too, had worry etched over her kind face.

It was because of him that they stood now at the threshold to his room.

"It will be most difficult," thought Henry, "To convince them of my ruse, but I have no choice. My path is set on a course I cannot change; only Beau knows of my real plan. I must convince them I am well."

With a deep breath, Henry raised his face to meet his friend's eyes, and from across the room, while still resting in bed, he welcomed them, "Please, come in. Thank you for coming."

As Walt and Louisa came to stand by his bed, Old Sam rushed to find two chairs that they could sit in while visiting with Henry at his bedside.

Once convinced Henry was settled against his pile of pillows and Walt and Louisa were comfortable, the large man took the dinner tray away and left them alone in the room.

It was Walt that spoke first, as his weary and worried eyes perused over Henry. "You cannot imagine how grieved we have been since Miss Louisa received from Doctor Hendrix about the terrible event that has befallen not only you, but Miss Emma. And grieved doubly so by the knowledge it was by your hand, Henry. By your hand!"

Walt shook his head in disbelief, his heavy heart struggling too much to continue.

Louisa took Henry's hand in hers. The sadness in her eyes was almost too much for him to bear seeing.

"Help us to understand," she softly begged. "Walt and I are here for you, no matter what. We share in your pain, so tell us Henry and please know you are among friends, who will not judge you." She feigned a smile then, the worry not leaving her face as Henry struggled to tell them his reasoning for coming after John, without revealing his true plan.

Henry lay back upon his pillows and sighed deeply, preparing to win over his audience.

"Friends, whom I have shared so much with," he expounded, "we have shared the pain of wounded, of watching the dying leave this earth. Their screams are forever etched in my soul." He watched as his meaningful words settled, the memories of all they endured in their eyes.

"That is a mark upon me that will never be wiped away, yet I am grateful for the ones who I could help, albeit now so many live on without an arm or a leg or a way to make a living for their families. The poor souls."

Henry continued speaking, heedless of his guests, gladly sharing at least that part of himself that he could, the part of the suffering and the experience all three shared together.

"And so here now my friends, I am bereft that you have travelled all the way to Richmond here to visit me. And yes, I am vividly aware of the nature of your visit and I must beg now for you to understand that the fury that ailed me has passed."

He saw no forgiveness, yet.

"There is no excuse for my actions, from running after Miss Emma and her John, and for drawing a gun on John and the accidental shooting of our dear Miss Emma as she bent to assist her husband. I have no excuse for this action, or even the action of the attempt on my own life, but it was with the knowledge I thought I had killed Miss Emma that I turned the gun on myself."

"I thought at that moment, I took the most innocent of lives, someone I had known since boyhood and yes, I admit loved as well. And that I should die as a consequence to that most grievous act. And so I awoke, much to my surprise, with a terrible non-fatal gunshot wound to the temple and Emma with a minor shoulder wound, and there was no threat to her baby."

It was Louisa who gasped then and asked, "Henry, a baby? Emma and John are expecting?" She placed her hand over her heart all the while saying, "Oh thank God, oh thank God for that!"

Before Louisa could speak any further, Henry interjected, "And as for my belief that this John Singer is really John Wilkes Booth, I have let that fury pass as well. It is inconceivable that assassin escaped his fate at the Garrett barn some two months ago."

They were both listening.

"As for the diary Old Sam claimed to have seen, without seeing it myself, I cannot believe it was of importance."

That statement seemed to carry weight, but Henry added to his performance.

"Emma would not marry a murderer! If this John Singer is shrouded in mystery, perhaps he is entitled to his privacy. Many in the war have stories they do not enjoy telling. Maybe one day we will come to understand more of his background and lineage. I only ask that you forgive me for all that I have wrought, I am truly sorry."

Henry bowed his head in a sorrowful gesture.

It was then Walt leaned over, "The war has taken so much from all of us. It is with my deepest hope that you are now healing, letting go. I have faith you will come back to us. Your past behavior is very worrisome, but it is a great joy to know you are repentant."

"I am a changed man, to be sure."

Walt nodded, accepting that. "Miss Louisa and I will pay a call to the Dixon residence and check on our Emma and her John. I will also write to Doctor Hendricks and advise him to return to Richmond when he can. And hopefully, soon you will take your place at the hospital in Alexandria with those poor suffering souls that need you."

Henry lifted his eyes to Walt and stared deeply into them in understanding. He tilted his head and said evenly and gently to his wise friend.

"It is true. I am so sorry for all I have done. I only want to be forgiven and yes, take my rightful place back in Alexandria. I know I am so terribly needed. I must apologize to Emma and John and ask their forgiveness."

Louisa had tears in her eyes. "Henry, you cannot believe how very worried we have been. Please, now look me in the eye and vow that you mean all the words you just said. Promise you are repentant and willing to move on. Remember, how you helped me when Jack died?"

"Of course. That was a time of great sorrow."

"It is a bond that will tie us as friends here on earth and in heaven."

Henry shifted his gaze to Louisa and saw the worry and grief in her eyes. For a moment he wanted to tell her the truth, admit that he was faking his change of heart and that he had just written to the soldier who gave him the gun to kill John Singer.

Instead he innocently said, "I'm sorry. I vow I am a changed man. Please, forgive me."

A slight smile touched her lips as she nodded and squeezed his hand. "I am so happy to hear you say that. Yes, you are forgiven."

"Thank you."

Walt then stood up, "Miss Louisa and I will stay a few more days. Rest well, and good night." Then Walt and Miss Louisa took their leave. He did it. They believed him. Now, to find that diary. And get rid of the man keeping him from Emma. Satisfied with his performance, Henry closed his eyes and slept.

CHAPTER FOURTEEN

Homestead of Beau Jackson in Durham, North Carolina

"I'm coming Doc. I'm coming to Richmond."
~~ CSA Sergeant Beau Jackson

It was early evening. The young man stood outside a cabin that showed neglect and disrepair, all due to his absence while serving in the war. He felt sullen; surveying what was left of his small but once prosperous tobacco farm. Where once stood several barns filled with tobacco drying in the hot summer sun, only one stood, the contents of the barn lay empty, only the distant odor of tobacco remained in the heavy wet heat of dusk. General Sherman's troops had left their destructive mark. He signed then wondering how he would support his family his wife and little daughter with one arm gone and no one to help with his fields. He surveyed a little patch of earth that had taken him all day to overturn and sighed.

But Beau Jackson knew he was luckier than most that survived the war, for his arm may be gone but at least he had a home. He still had his beloved wife Cora Lee and daughter Marianna. All those poor boys, he reminisced marching up the firing line of battle, some disappearing forever as the enemy bullets ripped them apart, their destroyed bodies unrecognizable in the aftermath.

Sometimes even now, at the onset of dusk his thoughts went back to those most horrid of days. Especially impossible to forget was his first battle, Bull Run that happened in Manassas, Virginia on July 21 of 1861. He remembered how proud he was to be part of the Confederate States of America, C.S.A.

The battle lines had wavered back and forth between the Union and Confederate lines all day. It was a hard fought battle. It wasn't until he saw the great general Stonewall Jackson mounted on his horse crossing the line of heavy fire with no fear in him that rallied his division with renewed energy to charge that hill and take the day.

He could almost hear General Bee calling out through the heavy fire, "There stands Jackson, standing like a Stonewall!"

The young man then opened his eyes remembering the last words of the great general as he lay dying from the complications of the amputation of his left arm at the Battle of Chancellorsville on May 10th, of 1863 and was heard to say "Let us cross over the river and rest under the shade of the tree."

He shook his head to disperse his thoughts as sadness gripped his heart. The general was dead two years now, the South defeated, his life and his future now forever changed.

The stillness of that moment was broken as the thundering gallop of a horse came closer and closer still to the small cabin. The young man ran to the front of the house wondering who it was come clamoring up the long drive to his secluded farm.

He began to hear his name echo through the thicket of trees, "Sergeant Jackson! A letter for you!"

The rider came closer finally enough to see clearly. It was Samuel Williams, the young son of the postmaster of Durham, the postmaster who died at the Battle of Cold Harbor Virginia June, 1864. The young boy jumped from his mount running up to the Sergeant holding his arm out with a letter gripped in his hand and said breathlessly, "See here Sergeant, it's a letter for you that came, all the way from Richmond."

Pleased with his delivery of the letter, the young boy smiled showing even white teeth, his stature not yet filled out from boyhood. His face was freckled and tanned from the summer sun, his eyes bright with hope of youth.

Beau held out his hand, wet and grimy from the day's labor and then asked quizzically to the young man, "Richmond you say?"

The young man nodded his head in affirmation and said, "See here, it's from a Doctor Henry Bradley."

Immediately at the sound of that name, Beau reached for the letter and said to the young man, "Well now, Samuel, after this here long ride out to deliver this here letter, why don't you sit a spell. Go ahead inside and Cora Lee will fix something up for you. It won't be much I afraid to say, but you are welcome to it."

"Thank you, sir."

"I only ask that you wait while I write a reply to this here letter." Beau called out to his wife from the front of the house, "Cora Lee, we have a guest."

With that a young and comely woman emerged from the house. Her plain shapeless dress was thin and worn and her feet were bare. Her long dark hair twined in a thick braid down her back, a young girl trailing behind her mother carrying a corncob doll in her hand her other hand grasping the skirt of her mother.

"Can you see to young Samuel's comfort? He brought me a letter all the way from Richmond. I thought it neighborly to have him rest and have something to eat while I read this here letter."

"Richmond?" asked his wife. "A letter all the ways from Richmond?" Her eyes widened in excitement and surprise all the while wondering who this could be from.

Anxious to read the letter, Beau said to his wife, "I'll tell yer more later, please see to Samuel's comfort. Marianna, help your mama now."

The little girl nodded to her father and silently followed her mother into the house.

Samuel smiled as the smell of fresh baked bread and coffee greeted him as he crossed the threshold. Young Samuel was barely in the house when Beau tore at the letter; wondering what it was the Doctor could want from him.

Beau unfolded the letter. With each word read, he felt his muscles stiffen, his teeth clamped tight to his jaw, and his blood turn ice cold even in the sweltering night. He knew what needed to be done.

Dear Sergeant Jackson:

I hope above all hope this finds you well, you wife and little girl the same. And of course good thoughts that perhaps your farm was spared when the burning of the Atlanta commenced, and then to the Carolinas in the path of General Sherman's Union forces. I only hope you and your family were spared such misery.

I write this to request a favor. I am here in Richmond, VA at my parents' home, resting and eating and healing the pain that which affects my aching heart.

You see I remember your parting words to me at the hospital in Alexandria, when you slipped the derringer in my hand and told me "some people just need killin." Ah how perceptive you were.

Your former hospital mate, John Singer, is most definitely a fraud, a fake and a murderer. Evidence exists. And by his ghostly cryptic actions, I know this man is in hiding.

John Singer is John Wilkes Booth, yes Booth the actor! Old Sam saw the diary containing papers and news clippings, documents that point to his true identity.

We will obtain that diary and take it to Washington, to prove that he is an imposter. The wrong man was killed at Garrett's barn. And then we will witness as the hand of the government reaches out, silences once and for all the man known as John Singer. And you and I will be lauded as the bravest of all men. Then Emma will be mine.

Think hard on this, Beau. But keep in your mind's eye the ones who died so horribly, the men you heard burning to death in the thick brush of the Battle of the Wilderness, screaming as they died. Do you think this imposter would ever have sacrificed so much, like they did? Never.

No one knows of this plan. All here in Richmond are still weighing my change of heart, the one from addled killer to gentle repentance. Only you know the truth in this way I keep my deception complete as I carefully calculate and consider Singer's next move. Steady my friend, your time to help in our retribution is near.

Write me soon and come to Richmond.

Doc

Beau stood motionless, the letter gripped tightly in his hand. He remembered his days in the Alexandria hospital ward next to the man with the broken leg, the intense black eyes, and the last encounter with him before leaving for Durham. He nodded his head and a slow deliberate smile crossed his face and knew what needed to be done.

"That's right Doc, that's right," he murmured to himself, "Some people just need killin. I'm coming, Doc. I'm coming to Richmond."

CHAPTER FIFTEEN

The Dixon Residence in Richmond, Virginia

"Annabelle, I am returning to Richmond."
~~ Doctor Jonas Hendrix

The late afternoon sun seemed to blaze without mercy into the great drawing room where Annabelle Dixon found herself pacing. The large windows were still devoid of coverings; the glass covered in soot and grime did little to cut the stifling heat and humidity of the late June afternoon. It was only after hearing the call of her youngest daughter Abby that pulled her attention away from the sullen appearance of this once grand room and her startling revelation of her son-in-law, John.

Within moments of hearing Abby's call to her, the girl raced into the drawing room, her white muslin dress patched together from remnants of one of Emma's old dresses, now made to fit her growing body.

"Why are you running in this heat, what have you been up too? Look child, your face is turning red, where you out without your bonnet?" Annabelle brushed one hand over her daughter's sweet face, the cheeks clearly flushed from the sun.

"I'm sorry, Mother. I was just outside. I saw some flowers out back by the stable. They were so pretty, see I picked them just for you!"

With that said Abby pulled her arms front to show her mother the tiny white Lily of the Valley flowers she had just picked.

"See, Mother, these are for you."

Annabelle bent down to receive the flowers as she did so her heart burst forth with love. Abby was so kind and gentle so like her father thought Annabelle, infinitely kind. She thought then of the difference of her and Emma who was headstrong and decisive. She remembered the day Emma told her that she was going to work at the hospital at Alexandria to help the soldiers, as she felt duty bound to help. And so she did.

The whole time Annabelle had hoped she would return, but stayed throughout the whole war. Now she had come home to Richmond. With John. She sighed, weighted with infinite trouble and pain as her future.

"May I please go see Emma and sit with her?"

Annabelle smiled past her troubled thoughts and said, "Yes dear, just please go easy. She may be resting."

Abby then said, "Oh I will go and pick more flowers for her too. It will make her happy! And I will pick some for John too; he said I was powerful pretty, just like Emma!"

As she was ready to leave the room Abby paused a moment, surveyed the great room where bouquet of flowers used to be on display, daily. "Mother, will it ever be like it was, before the war came? I miss Father and Caleb."

Annabelle reached for her youngest child and hugged her close. She said simply, "Abby, I miss your father and Caleb to so very much, every single day. We must be grateful that we have each other and we are together." She stroked Abby's blond strands of hair and held her tight. She then said in an effort to dispel the moment of sadness, "Don't forget your bonnet when you pick more flowers child. Your mother loves you."

With those words said, Abby turned and left the room.

Annabelle then sat down on the dilapidated couch clenching the flowers in her hands wondering of all that had befallen her family.

She knew that she now shared a very dangerous secret with Emma but one that she could not reveal, and that was the true identity of her husband John. The danger enhanced doubly by old family friend Henry Bradley who rants could only incite a possible investigation of her family. And what then she thought? What then?

A knock on the cherry drawing doors interrupted her thoughts as Esmeralda appeared with a letter in hand and politely approached the mistress of the house.

Esmeralda came forward; even the servant seemed to notice there was a palpable sadness that surrounded her. "See here Mrs. Dixon, I have a letter for you, just brought by courier." She extended her hand to deliver the letter. "Maybe this here letter will cheer you."

Mrs. Dixon extended her hand to receive the letter noticing the return address as Alexandria and a slow smile managed to creep to her lips. "Oh Esmeralda, I guess I was just reminiscing is all, missing my William and Caleb. Thank you kindly for the letter, rest your mind. I am fine, and yes," she swallowed hard to her next words, "Emma is recovering, John is her new husband and we will have a child here in this house."

Esmeralda then turned to leave and stopped suddenly. She then turned back to her mistress and stated plainly, "You know I jest think I seen Mr. John somewhere before, but I just can't figure it! Well never mind, he is sure 'nough part of the family now!"

She then left the room as Mrs. Dixon sat on the tattered sofa to read the letter from Jonas, the same tattered sofa where a few weeks ago he had made his intentions known. She tore it open and began to read...

Dearest Annabelle,

It is with a heart steeped with thoughts of you that I pen to you all that is happening here in Alexandria.

As you know most of the soldiers that were ambulatory have gone home, the many that are too sick still remain here in my care. I can't help but think back just a short time ago as our soldiers left this hospital with an arm or a leg missing and wonder still how they will make a living to help their families.

I try yet I cannot help but wonder and despair for those who were farmers or blacksmiths or bricklayers that will be forced to try to work without sufficient limbs to support the work that fed their families and housed them from the elements. What of them, Annabelle?

It grieves me so. For some the war took their lives, for others it took their livelihoods. I have only now to try to help those soldiers here and now through illnesses that perhaps they might never recover from.

I have heard from our friend Walt Whitman that Henry seems to be recovering from his confused mental state and that his head wound is also sufficiently healing.

I met with Henry before coming to Alexandria and it does seem to me he is indeed repentant for all he wrought on our dear Emma and her husband John.

That he has given up this crazy notion of your John being John Wilkes Booth.

Have to admit Annabelle that there is something about your John that does not set right with me, but I do believe that perhaps there was some kind of shell shock that assailed him and his cryptic ways and manners are all part of that incident.

In any case, I think now this can be put to rest. And perhaps now with Emma on her way to recovery and the baby coming we can plan for happier events in the future. And, Annabelle I do hope that you will consider me a part of future happier events.

This war has taken so much from us all, your husband and your son and my wife too. And with what was taken from us cannot be duplicated ever again, but we can look to each other to share our grief and loss and try to find solace and care in one another.

It is my greatest hope dear Annabelle.

*It is night time presently, and my thoughts stray to our
parting in the foyer of your home, the feel of your soft cheek
against my lips and I hear a nightingale sing, perhaps calling
to their beloved to come home.*

*With that in mind, please accept my humble attempts to
put into words what my heart is feeling about you.*

> *The nightingale that sings her song*
> *Of loves lost and so forlorn*
> *That remind me of a time gone by*
> *Gone now that make me cry*
> *And so I think of your beautiful face*
> *Set before me with such grace*
> *That reach for me and my heart*
> *Stay with me now please not to part*
> *For perhaps it can be true please tell me so*
> *That you could love me - I beg to know*

*I will be returning to Richmond forthwith, as we now have
physicians ready to stead my place. I also hope upon my
return that Henry will be sufficiently recovered to run this
hospital and take his rightful place as a dedicated and skilled
Doctor.*

I shall call on you upon my arrival.
You must forgive my boldness,
Jonas

Annabelle clenched the letter in her hand. Her eyes that were
brimming with tears finally gave over her and spilled onto the letter
staining it with her broken heart.

Jonas is such a dear and kind man, such comfort he has brought.
Yet she knew she must keep the truth of John from him, a secret
locked away in the well springs of her heart.

"How grievous this situation is for all of us!" She muttered aloud,
pacing the floor as she thought, speaking as through he could hear.
"Jonas forgive me, for as I enter into what I hope to be a comforting
presence in my life, I already am bound not to share this secret with
you, for to do so may endanger you as well. You say Henry has had a
change of heart? Why such a sudden change in him? I don't buy it. I
don't. He could be feigning this recant for something more devious
and dangerous. He bears watching."

"And what of John Wilkes Booth? The world thinks he is dead but
he lives as John Singer. I fear there will be a calamity coming and I
can do nothing to stop it."

Annabelle signed as she still clenched the letter in her hand. She climbed the staircase to go rest on her bed, her footsteps echoing on the marble and bare floors, each step she thought, bringing her closer to the unspoken storm yet to come.

———— ◆ ————

The stunning revelation from John's new mother-in-law as to his true identity shook his usual confident demeanor. He could not tell Emma that her mother was wise as to who he was and what he had done.

"That diary," lamented John under his breath, "That diary has once again exposed me. Yet, I cannot burn it. I cannot destroy it, to do that would forever deny my true self and my actions." He shook his head slightly. "We must go to Tudor Hall," he thought, "To my family they will help us."

John stood at the top of the stairs and fumbled with the collar of his shirt. He then pulled up the gold medallion from around his neck and squeezed it tight. It was the Angus Dei that Asia gave him. "Help me Asia," he murmured under his breath as he strode down the hallway where Emma was resting. "Help me."

His wife slept. John stood silent as he watched Emma resting peacefully. He sat in a chair beside her and gazed at her face. He felt so fortunate to not only be alive, but to have her to love. He murmured under his breath, "Please God, do not ever let us be parted."

He then heard Emma softly call his name. John gently leaned over and watched Emma's fluttering green eyes open and remove the traces of sleep from her sight. "I am so sorry, my darlin' to disturb you, please go back to sleep and rest."

Emma shifted her weight in the bed to face him fully and said, "I heard you say something just now. Don't you know, dear husband. that we shall never be parted?"

John grasped her hand and held it to his lips. "Emma, if only that were true."

His thoughts rambled through his mind. He heard the threatening words of from Annabelle in his ears, the words of Doctor Hendrix, the close proximity of Henry Bradley and his ramblings against him. The fact that Emma's mother knew his name was too much at that moment as he felt the truth of his true identity was inching closer to being exposed.

"Emma, we must try to get to Tudor Hall as soon as you are able to travel. We must leave Richmond. It is time now to begin our journey in flight and try to find a corner on this earth to live in peace. I feel it be a life full of peril, fit for me and my crime, but what of you dear wife? What crime have you committed to be placed in such a horrible condition as life on the run, with a murderer? For no matter how repentant I am, that is who I am, that is why I will never burn that diary.”

“Those diaries that exposed my true identity to you and could again betray me sometime in our near future. Only now with more at stake, you and our child.”

“John,” asked Emma, her voice wavering slightly, “Has something happened? Did you have your visit with mother?”

John held his breath for a moment and smiled at his wife, “Why of course we did. It was very nice, indeed. You must not concern yourself with that, why Annabelle and I are the greatest of friends.”

“You can’t imagine how very happy I am to hear that,” she smiled, “But what shall I tell mother about us leaving and what shall I tell her where we will be going? She will need to know.”

John thought about this carefully before he answered and said to his wife, “This will be hard for you and for her, but we cannot tell her about our plans to go to Tudor Hall or where we will go from there. I am sorry. It will be the end for us if we do. Such is the life now that is set before us. I will understand if you cannot do this.”

The tears gleamed in Emma’s blue eyes, as she knew even before John has answered her that in committing to a life in hiding, she would be leaving all she knew behind, forever.

“I will never leave you, John, never. No matter what.”

He kissed her lips then, gently and sweetly, laid her down to rest. He looked down at her and said simply. “I love you, Emma.”

◆

It was only a few days later when the letter came from Asia. All was in place for John and Emma’s flight to Tudor Hall, there they would decide the uncertain future for the young family.

As per Asia’s instructions they were to leave Richmond immediately and arrive under the semblance of night.

The last part of Asia’s letter strongly advised of telling no one of their plans for that would endanger the entire family. John realized it would now mean that Emma would be from this point forward forever parted from her family. For to tell them, however innocent, could bring certain death to them all.

CHAPTER SIXTEEN

Aurora Farm in Martinsburg, Virginia
December, 1865

"Our darling Juliet has been born"
~~ John Wilkes and Emma Dixon Booth

The summer heat and humidity seemed to linger indefinitely, but eventually gave way to a chill of autumn and the onset of winter. An early cold snap in the weather chilled the air as Emma's confinement came to an end. With her time nearing, John had secured the services of a midwife to help Emma with the birth of their child.

The baby was born with the advent of Christmas upon them. Emma's good health and strong vitality procured a safe birth. It was a girl, and they named her Juliet, as promise so many months ago, a promise that was fulfilled upon the appearance into the world of this beautiful child.

It seemed to John all of life stood still as he gazed into the tiny face of his baby girl. He looked around at the modest yet comfortable home he shared with Emma and smiled. He remembered first seeing this place, named Aurora for the Roman goddess of dawn and how fitting that name was for their new life together. It had really been a beautiful new beginning.

The clapboard and whitewashed structure had modest furnishings, with a barn and field around it that would hopefully produce after spring plantings. The lands escaped the burning of Union General Sheridan in the spring of '65; they were fortunate to have land that may yield a future harvest. And, so this was home now to the little family with the horrific secret.

John swaddled the newborn and caressed her silken cheek while Emma lay propped on pillows, exhausted and pale after a giving birth, but to John she had never looked more beautiful.

The baby began to fuss. "Bring her here," Emma said, "she may be hungry." Handing over Juliet to her mother, he watched silently as the child began to nurse from her mother's breast, all the while Emma's face beaming with love and joy.

John sat in a chair beside the bed, savoring the first moments of his daughter's innocent life. He felt overwhelmed by love. It warmed his chest, burned so deep he had to put it into words.

"I love you, dearest Emma. You deserve so much more than this modest home, things I cannot give you, only this life on the run and the uncertainty of each day."

Emma held baby Juliet, keeping the fragile infant swaddled to stay warm on the chilly night. "I have the man I love and a beautiful daughter. I need nothing else to be happy."

For a while he simply watched, in awe of how pure and new their newborn looked. Juliet had been blessed with delicate feminine features and soft golden hair that made her pale skin seem luminous. Her tiny fingers clenched the edge of the blanket.

"Look how beautiful she is," Emma admired their daughter, memorizing her face. "Look at her lashes, they are curled up, long and black like yours."

"Perhaps she has my eyes."

Emma smiled at the hopeful thought, "Come Juliet, open your eyes so your mother who loves you can see them." The baby fussed a little, made noises, but did not cry. She stretched both hands, gripping the blanket in those tiny fingers and began to nurse once again. Soon it was clear she had fallen asleep.

She never opened her eyes, not once. Emma's voice became fearful, "She never opened her eyes, I can't see her eyes!"

John's blood froze cold as he realized in the hours since her birth, he too had not seen their baby open her eyes, but dismissed it readily for Emma's sake.

"Don't worry yourself, darling. She's tired. I'm sure being born was difficult. All is just fine. She will open them tomorrow. Now rest and grow strong again. I will care for her while you sleep."

As Emma surrendered Juliet into his arms, the tiny body wrapped inside the blanket seemed so fragile. Holding her brought an ache to John's heart. Everything about the pregnancy had been risky, from the day Emma suffered so much blood loss after her shoulder injury, to the long ride on the old buckboard from Tudor Hall, to working so hard trying to make the farm inhabitable.

As he held his newborn daughter fear suddenly gripped his heart. He tried not to give into the possibility, but what if he thought,

What if she were blind?

Was this the punishment the heavens decided to bestow upon his family, punishing an innocent child for the sins of her father? Yet inside his troubled soul John feared the answer.

"Juliet," he whispered, rocking her gently in his arms. The ache inside was so deep, he couldn't bear to lay her down in the cradle. He had to touch her, to feel how real she was.

"I love you, my darling."

Heaven help her please, he felt tears sting his eyes. He vowed to do anything, and everything to protect his child. And begged the Almighty to let her see.

This same scene repeated itself until the third day when the miracle happened, ensuring to mother and father, the special gift that was their child, Juliet. The new parents were heartsick. Three days passed without Juliet opening her eyes. Emma was horrified that her baby might be blind. John too feared she had no sight, yet tried to sooth Emma as best as he could, as her agony was more than he could bear.

On the third day, Emma lay on the bed sobbing, her joy at the birth mere days ago gone. She had tried once again to get the baby to open her eyes, failing. It was too much for John to witness. He refused to believe that God would find a way to spare his life, give him a second chance with a wife and a child, only to have Juliet burdened with blindness.

John stood by the cradle and picked her up. He swaddled the baby, speaking softly to his child, almost willing her to see. "Open your eyes, daughter of mine. Look at your father, the one who loves you more than my life itself, open your eyes for me and see me." Juliet snuggled and cooed, hearing his voice. Her eyelids gently fluttered. He watched her struggle to open them. He called her name gently, "Juliet, open your eyes, child, come now and look upon your father. I love you so."

Juliet slowly opened her eyes to gaze at her father. She smiled. As John moved, her eyes followed his face. The baby sighed with contentment, unaware something extraordinary had just transpired. "Emma, look! She can see! Our Juliet can see. Oh, just look at her magnificent eyes!"

She was not blind.

Emma jumped up, running to John who was all at once crying and rejoicing. "Her eyes, dear husband, are exactly like yours!"

He admired his daughter, looking into the exact same eyes as his, eyes so black it was like they had no iris, all at once compelling and breathtakingly beautiful.

John reached into his shirt, and pulled out from it the Agnus Dei, the metal that had protected him. It had identified him to Asia, proving he lived and was her brother. He took it off his neck to lay it around Juliet's.

He then said to his wife, "This medal has protected me when in the hospital in Alexandria, to the drawing room of your family's house in Richmond where Asia first saw me, and now to the joy in Juliet's health. If anything should happen to me, remind our daughter of her father's love. Tell her, if she ever needs me, to hold it and call my name and I will come to her."

John placed the gleaming gold medal around Juliet's neck and watched as the baby place her tiny hand on the medal, where it rested directly upon her heart.

◆

Within weeks of Juliet's birth, as motherhood warmed her heart, Emma realized the pain she must have caused her mother leaving Richmond all those months ago, sneaking out of the house in the middle of the night with no note to her family. She understood a mother's love, the agony she had caused and regretted it.

Now as a mother herself she wrestled with the suffering she caused her mother. "She is a grandmother and she doesn't even know it. I could be dead and she would not know it." She lamented to herself, "Oh Mother forgive me!"

Emma gazed at the cradle where little Juliet lay smiling sweetly at her mother, her dark black eyes almost staring through her, and she realized what she must do.

Against all she knew was right and safe, she began to write.

December 20, 1865
Mrs. Annabelle Dixon
Richmond Virginia

Dearest Mother, I ask forgiveness for leaving you and Abby last July without a word or letter.

As a mother now I can understand the suffering this has caused you and I grieve that I cannot alleviate your pain. Yes, our daughter Juliet Annabelle Singer was born December 17 and is healthy and beautiful.

I cannot tell you where we are I can only tell you that we are all well. Circumstances that I cannot share with you prevent me from sharing anything further. I cannot say anything more. Please do not tell anyone you have heard from me. Forgive me.

Your devoted daughter
Emma

Emma sealed the letter, remembering not to put a return address on the envelope, only wanting to let her mother know she was fine and that her granddaughter Juliet was born and was healthy. She was sure no one would be able to find them.

CHAPTER SEVENTEEN

The Dixon Residence in Richmond, Virginia

"The time has come at last"
~~ Henry Bradley

The months had crawled by interminably as Henry waited for Beau to reach Richmond. But he had sent word to Richmond, a letter explaining all. The man's wife had been sick. Cora Lee was his world. Beau could not leave her and his little girl, Marianna, until she was well.

The advent of Christmas was fast approaching as Henry impatiently waited for the arrival of his former patient and helpmate in ridding the world of a traitor.

Over the months that had passed Henry had been quite successful in his ruse to convince all those who were around him that he was indeed repentant for his earlier behavior and attack on Emma's husband John.

Walt and Louisa had left at the end of that previous summer, their minds at ease with his heartfelt change of heart. Their friendship was solidified.

Yet, all the while the seeds of revenge grew deeper and deeper within him. The letter that finally arrived saying Beau was on his way now a comfort to him as he laid plans to confront John, take the diary from him and kill him.

Even after Henry heard the news from months agon that John and Emma had left her mother's house in the middle of the night, he kept true to his task. Knowing they had gone into hiding did little to dampen his spirits now, for he knew somehow, some way, he would find their hiding place and go after them.

Nothing fazed Henry, not even the news that Annabelle Dixon and Jonas Hendrix had found favor with each other and were planning to marry after the New Year.

He figured Annabelle must know where Emma is, and he would find a way to somehow get Annabelle to tell hm.

"After all," thought Henry, "She has nothing to fear from me, as I am a totally changed man!"

With that he tossed his head back and laughed the sinister laughter, the sound of it cutting through the silence of his room, the bareness and emptiness of the bedroom echoing the strange and menacing sounds.

With the thought of Beau's impending arrival Henry decided to pay a call to the Dixon House.

He had only seen Doctor Hendrix over the passing months a few times to discuss business and the timetable to his taking over the Hospital in Alexandria. Henry agreed to go, but only after the wedding and more importantly, he thought, "Only after I find out where Booth is hiding, and Beau is here in Richmond."

It was with that goal in mind that Henry left his bedroom and walked the length of the upstairs hallway to the top of the stairs. The echo of his shoes on the marble floor seemed to his over-active imagination, reminiscent of cannon fire, so loud were his footsteps on the barren floors as he make his way to the foyer.

He looked around the lower rooms and into the great parlor to see if Old Sam would like to accompany him on the short ride to the Dixon household.

Not finding him inside Henry wandered about the back of the house, where half of a barn that was barely standing and blackened by soot stood. It had once housed a fine carriage, a team of the finest horses and a vast array of other healthy animals. He sighed remembering better times.

It was then Old Sam appeared at his side, almost as if he could anticipate Henry's next move.

The big man smiled and asked, "What yer doing out her for Doc? You needin somptin?"

"As a matter of fact, I do" said Henry with a smile back to his friend, "How about we hitch up that nag we got and take a ride to the Dixon house and have a visit. I haven't seen Jonas in a few weeks and with Christmas coming up and the wedding soon after, it might be good to pay a call."

Old Sam flashed his toothy grin, "It makes me powerful happy to see youse back to being youse good old self. I is just so glad you all good now. And yes suh, I be happy to hitch up that horse and we'll head right over there."

The ride to the Dixon house pulled at Henry's heart.

A dilapidated buggy now served as his carriage; with each step the old nag of a horse pulled him past house after house in varying degrees of disrepair. It broke his heart as he remembered happier times riding this same street visiting neighbor after neighbor each house more ornate than the last.

And finally to the Dixon house, remembering the time right before the war, the coming out party of beautiful Emma, the talk he had with Emma's father as permission was given to court her.

He closed his eyes and in his mind he saw her once again in her blue gown with pearls wrapped about her magnificent blond hair like a crown. She looked like a princess, thought Henry, who was waiting to claim him as her prince.

Henry and Old Sam climbed out of the dilapidated buggy and walked up past the broken cobblestone driveway to the front of the house. The French double doors once pristine white that were the focal point of the entrance to their grand home were still covered in black soot with remnants of gunshot holes visible here and there through the door. "My God," thought Henry. "One can only imagine what could have happened here."

With that solemn thought, Henry turned the brass chime on the door to announce their arrival. The echo the chime made seem to resonate throughout the empty home reminding all those who enter of its former glory.

The moment was quickly dispelled as Annabelle Dixon ran to the front door herself to greet her guest. Henry was only mildly surprised at Annabelle coming to the door as he remembered all that remained of the Dixon help was Esmeralda and Charles.

Much like his own home, everyone now did things they never would have done before the war. Decorum and social status were a thing of the past. He sighed remembering that he must keep up the ruse of repentance.

"Never more so," he thought, "Than with Emma's mother."

Annabelle acknowledged Henry and Old Sam as she gestured with her hands in a welcoming yet cool manner.

She had never spoken to him about what he had done, acted like it never happened, and even stranger he thought never mentioned what and why Emma and John left so suddenly or where they were for that fact he thought.

"She must know," mused Henry, "She must know where they are. I must try to find out! I must!"

Henry smiled carefully mindful to keep his countenance sweet and inviting as he said to his hostess, "Thank you, Mrs. Dixon. It was kind of you to greet us. I heard of your impending nuptials. Sam and I are happy for you. It is our most heartfelt hope to sit with you and Jonas, to pay our respects for your upcoming wedding."

Annabelle nodded back at both the men in her foyer and said, "Henry, thank you to you, and to Old Sam. "Come then into the front parlor and I will find Jonas."

With that said she led Henry and Old Sam into the parlor and quickly excused herself to find Jonas, who apparently stayed here quite regularly now.

Henry took stock of the once beautiful room, the same parlor where he approached Mr. Dixon about his courting Emma, the same front parlor where Emma married Booth.

It will right itself sure enough. He would right it. "Emma loves me," thought Henry as he walked about the shabby room, "She came to me and told me that she loves me, not John. She begged me to come and find her. And when I do, we shall live as man and wife and the child she has will bear my name not his."

He smiled as he remembered this, then stopped suddenly, his feet anchored to the floor his breath became shallow, as he noticed a letter on a side table next to the stained horsehair couch a letter with a distinctive cursive writing he knew as Emma's.

He focused his eye on the letter and saw no return address on it yet continued to visually survey the letter; he focused wholly on the postmark,

Martinsburg, Virginia! He found them at last!

CHAPTER EIGHTEEN

Aurora Farm in Martinsburg, Virginia

"You are wrong Henry, my name is Mrs. John Singer."
~~Emma Dixon Singer

Emma, John and baby Juliet were relaxing by the warm fire that was nicely heating the small farmhouse. Night had fallen and the chill outside from the December winter air prompted John to fetch additional wood to burn in the fireplace. He felt driven to protect and help his wife and newborn baby girl.

As he slipped on his overcoat, he heard riders coming near. Alarm coursed through his veins.

This house and location were fairly isolated and riders were scarce. He stepped away from the door, wishing it were stronger, not just simple paneled wood.

There wasn't even a strong lock on it.

Emma heard the hoof beats pounding too and stood, carefully lay the sleeping baby in her cradle, as alarm raced through her, as well.

"John, who is it? Who is coming, can you see?"

He peered through the curtain at the front window, but it was too dark to see who was approaching. A warning knot tightened inside, but he kept his voice even, careful not to cause Emma fear.

"No darlin' I can't see who it is. But try not to worry yourself; I'll take care of it."

With that said John reached into his black riding boots and pulled out a gun, the sound of his pulling back the hammer snapped through the usual peaceful quiet of the modest home.

John stepped away from the curtain, not wanting anyone to see him. Suddenly the galloping sounds from horses being ridden hard stopped and there was silence.

His mind flashed back to many months ago when he was trapped in the barn at Garrett's farm, his conspirator Davey Herold fast asleep, with his fellow conspirator who supplanted him James W. Boyd urging him to escape before it was too late.

He remembered the sound of his gun handle cocked and ready as he fled the barn into the night.

"Are they gone?" Emma hissed, "I don't hear anything!"

John turned to answer when suddenly the front door to the house burst open as someone kicked it open.

There stood Henry Bradley, a gun immediately aimed at John and he was followed by Beau Jackson, a man he recognized as his former hospital mate in Alexandria, and behind them stood Old Sam.

"I have found you at last, Booth," spewed Henry as John aimed his own gun back at him, perhaps the only think keeping the vengeance filled man from firing.

In his current state, it was clear Henry would be happy to shoot John down in cold blood.

"Here you are in hiding, with a life on the run, just like the coward you are. You could have saved all of us what will be a very sad scene here tonight if you had only died in that barn."

Henry marched into the small home that was now bursting with so many occupants, and said in a slow deliberate voice, all the while the gun never leaving the target of John's heart.

"You remember Sergeant Beau Jackson, right?"

He indicated the man with only one arm who stood behind him.

"Sergeant," was all John said.

"He met you at the hospital. He hates you, too. And he was kind enough to give me the derringer that I tried to kill you with last spring."

"I wondered where a physician would get a pistol," John kept his voice calm, his aim on Henry still.

"He told me 'some people just need killin'" and Henry laughed. "He gave me the gun as a farewell gift. Isn't that nice? I couldn't save his arm, but I saved his life. He knew you were a fake, just as I knew. And Old Sam knows too, isn't that right, Sam?"

The big man said nothing, his eyes wide, visibly stunned at the scene unfolding in front of him.

"It was just pure luck or perhaps my good fortune, Emma," he continued explaining his reasons for tracking them down, "that I paid a social call to your mother's house to pay my respects for her upcoming wedding to Jonas. Low and behold, right there on a table I spied a letter from you to your mother. I saw the postmark." He tapped his temple that now bore a large vertical scar, "But I'm a smart man. It was easy to track you down from that postmark; there isn't much left standing out here in Martinsburg." Henry smiled a sinister smile as he recounted his genius ability to uncover their lair.

Old Sam stood firmly by the door entrance, transfixed by Henry's behavior and said in an unsteady voice, "See here Doc, youse never tole me we was coming here, coming after Mister John again. Never tole me nothin' about this. Youse said we was visiting another soldier that needed some tending, and that soldier was a friend of this here, Sergeant Beau."

"Well, I lied."

"No Doc, this is wrong. You gots some very bad thoughts in your head now." Old Sam tried to reason with his friend. "Let's go b'fore things get out of hand. Let's leave Mister John and Emma and their baby in peace. No good can come from this here."

Henry laughed again, a peculiar cackling sound, and suddenly whirled around to face his faithful friend. It was then everyone witnessed the true insanity of the man holding the gun.

"No! He dies!"

"Not tonight."

Unable to argue anymore with Old Sam, he began to rant in nonsensical noises as the wild frenzy of revenge coursed through his body. His need for vengeance appeared as pure madness in the once gentle eyes of the now crazed lunatic who had sworn to kill John. He was wild, almost like a feral animal. He had even forgotten language, only making furious sounds.

Beau was clearly aware now this journey was not just about trying to expose this John Singer as a fake and a fraud to the world. Henry's objective was for something even more sinister.

He tried to reason with Henry who was flailing the gun all about the room, pointing it at John, then at Emma and even at the cradle with the now crying Juliet.

Hearing the baby cry, Beau stepped close and put his hand up, "Lower the gun, Henry. No one's getting' shot tonight. If we are here to take the diary that will expose this man as Booth, then let's get it and get out of here."

Henry in his madness shouted to Beau, "No, we'll take the diary and then kill this imposter. Yes, that is what we will do!"

Beau shook his head, "I thought I had the stomach for this, but seeing Miss Emma and her baby." He looked at the infant in the cradle who Henry was still swinging his gun toward, "I have a wife and little girl at home. I don't want to be part of any killin' here. Let's get the diary and get out."

Henry shoved at Beau, pushing him away and finally found the ability to speak right again. But his voice was shrill as he said in a crazed voice, "You are a coward! Don't you see he is Booth? Remember his fancy talk at the hospital and the fact he could not tell you what battle he fought in? Because he was never IN any battle. Somehow he escaped the Garrett barn and is hiding in plain sight. We cannot let him get away. He has to be killed."

"No, put down the gun."

Henry was adamant, "But Emma told me to find her and kill John so we could be together!"

"Henry," cried Emma. "What are you talking about? I never told you such a thing!"

He turned his attention to her, the gun still wavering in his hand, pointing it and shaking it. "My love." His eyes were glazed, as if only seeing pieces of reality. "Now Emma, tell them. Tell John tonight, right here in front of everyone, how you came to me. You said you wanted me, that you loved me, not him. Tell them that you wanted me to come and find you, to kill him so we could be together, and that baby will carry my name, not his."

She shook her head.

"Tell them Emma."

Again, she refused.

"Tell them right now," he begged, his voice shaky, "Tell them that in truth, your name is really Mrs. John Wilkes Booth. Let me hear you say it. Once it is said, I will kill him. It will be as if a cancer is eliminated from this earth."

Emma could not believe the words she was hearing from his mouth. All the while, she remained highly aware of the volatility of the situation. She felt fearful for John and her baby. She reached for Henry trying to get him to stop aiming the gun, "Come now. You know my name is Mrs. John Singer."

His feral snarling returned.

Emma lowered her hand.

She had seen and heard enough.

"This must stop, right now, Henry. You must know, deep inside, you know the truth. I never came to you." His head shook in denial. "I never asked you to kill John and marry me and be the father to Juliet. You know, deep inside, that is not true."

Henry screamed long and loud in pure rage as he intermittently pointed the gun, swinging his aim toward John then Emma.

He glanced at the baby, who had stopped crying and had her eyes open. His loud voice had frightened Juliet so much, she lay there too scared to make another sound.

"No! Stop with the lies, Emma! You came to me one night, in my room in Richmond, and told me to come for you. I am here now. I only want that diary to prove that he is Booth. Besides, killing him will be like killing a man who is supposedly dead. It won't matter."

The room stood still and silent.

Suddenly Henry pointed the gun right at the cradle, in a desperate craze moment.

Old Sam launched himself at Henry.

Their bodies slammed together.

Old Sam was twice the size of the crazed man. He wrestled the gun from Henry, slid it away to let it harmlessly clatter along the floor and yelled out, "Run Mister John! Run right now! I won't let nothin' happen here to an innocent baby."

John ran toward Emma, and she too yelled at him, "You must leave, right now! Run, John."

He kissed his wife, looked longingly one last time at Juliet and ran from the house. He was on his horse quickly.

Hearing John galloping away from house, Emma stood transfixed as each hoof beat took him further and further away.

Old Sam was still was wrestling with Henry.

He flipped him over on his stomach, arms and legs sprawled out on the wood floor. Then Old Sam pulled his full weight down on top of him and said "Get somethin' to tie him with I can't sit here fo'ever."

"There is rope beside the wood box," Emma volunteered.

Beau hurried, found a long piece of rope to help subdue him. Once they had his arms tied, they stood him upright again, standing with both men holding tight onto his arms.

Henry turned to Emma his eyes wild in madness, crying out, "The diary. Find the diary."

"I don't know what you are talking about, Henry."

"You do!" Then he shouted at Beau, "It will expose him as Booth. Find it. Kill him."

"No, Henry. No one is dying tonight."

The two men hoisted him up and carried Henry away, tied him to the saddle of his own horse. By then, all the fight had gone out of him. He sat listlessly, his eyes glazed, mumbling sounds no human ever should.

When they were done Old Sam returned and faced Emma, his big hulking form filling up the small house. He bent his head, making a heartfelt apology to her.

"See here Miss Emma, I didn't know any of this. Henry asked Beau to come up to Richmond to visit him. He did. Then they all decided to come here to Martinsburg to visit a fellow patient from the war." His lowered head shook in sadness and disbelief.

"I thought it was gonna be like a social call, another friend, you know? But I should'a known." He blamed himself for not seeing the truth. "Henry didn't want me to come, but I insisted cuz' I didn't want him making this trip on his own. He needs me."

"It's true, he does need you."

"I didn't know he still had such terrible evil on his mind. All along, he lied to me. He never was right in the head. Addled, through and through. I never seen such madness. I is powerful sorry."

Emma reached for the hulking man, laying her small hand upon the sleeve of his upper arm, offering her thanks. "Old Sam, you have served Henry well. It isn't your fault. None of it. No one could have stopped his insanity. But, you did stop him from hurting anyone tonight. You saved my baby. Thank you."

"It's the least I could do."

Hearing Juliet finally start to make normal fussing sounds, Emma turned and scooped up her precious child. Old Sam eyed the tiny girl, gave a smile.

"She sure pretty, Miss Emma."

"Thank you."

"Got your gold hair, but Mister John's dark eyes." Outside, they could hear Beau yelling at their hostage to be quiet.

"What are you going to do with him?"

"Well," he paused, listening unhappily to Henry's rantings. "I best be getting him back to his folks house. I think a hospital of some kind might be best, to help ease his mind."

"He cannot be free," Emma concurred, "For he cannot be trusted."

Sam gave a quick nod. From his viewpoint, he looked down on both Emma and over to Juliet lying in the cradle, who was peacefully sleeping again.

"Mister John's diary, that's what drove Henry mad." He declared, clicking his tongue in disgust. "We should have burned it that day, when you and me found it by the fire pit."

Emma didn't disagree. "Yes, perhaps we should have."

"Goodbye for now, Mrs. John Singer," said Sam, and as he turned to leave for the trip to Richmond he said in a whisper, "Goodbye, Mrs. John Wilkes Booth."

Emma stood by the threshold of the open door to the house as Beau also made his apologies to Emma. She stood all alone as she watched silently as the three riders left until the darkness swallowed them into the night.

CHAPTER NINETEEN

Somewhere near Santa Rosa, California
FOUR YEARS LATER

"My dearest child Juliet, I am coming home"
~~ John Wilkes Booth

Late winter, 1869.

The fire that blazed in the stone hearth in the log cabin home situated in the woods of California did little to warm the spirits of the lone man residing there.

Sitting near the fire in a straight back cane chair, he leaned toward the firelight to read, his fingers anxiously gripping the letter in his hands. The writing on the outside was familiar and the longing to see her beautiful face and embrace her warm body with his arms overwhelmed him in that moment of recollection.

He rubbed his thumb over the wax seal.

The words inside were for his eyes only.

He stood up suddenly and leaned upon the rough pine mantle as he tore open the sealed letter and read the words that would soon bring him to his knees.

> *My dearest John:*
>
> *The cold of winter is ebbing away now here in Richmond. I think perhaps we may have an early spring this year. With each and every passing season, every passing month and day, my longing for you increases tenfold. Yet, I take comfort in the knowledge that you are safe out there in hiding, my husband. It is this knowledge and this knowledge alone that allows me to continue on without you.*
>
> *Oh, how I wish you could see Abby now! She is fourteen and such a lovely young lady. I wish for her what I had, in those lovely days before the war. Fine dresses and parties and dancing. It is what every young woman wants.*
>
> *But there will be no cotillions or parties for her coming out, not even four years after the war. That life is gone. What was before, will never come again. My heart aches for her in this, but it is my most fervent hope that as we move forward as a family from this most darkest of times that a new beginning will be had, for all of us.*
>
> *Mother and Jonas continue to flourish, happy since their marriage in January of 1866. Jonas has proven to be a kind a*

gentle step-father, embracing our dear sweet Juliet as his own granddaughter.

Our family home here in Richmond is continuing to improve albeit slowly, with Jonas' help, of course. He is now fully committed to teaching medicine to young students at the University of Virginia in Charlottesville. With mother accompanying him, naturally, on the occasions when he is lecturing there.

Oh John, and to our darling child, Juliet. She is now four years old and is the center of joy in my life. I look at her and see your image in her sweet face. Her dark velvety eyes with the upturned black lashes, so beautifully rare, her expressions in those eyes matching her father's gaze to perfection.

She is becoming so aware of your absence now, as she grows up. She gazes at your picture and asks of me constantly "Where is my Papa?"

I am fearful that the vague answers I provide to her are not sufficient to ease the longing in her heart. It is as if she has reached into my own heart and is mirroring the longing I feel for you, dear husband. I miss you so.

I think of that winter night at the Aurora Farm, so long ago, when our own small family was forever changed. Seeing you leave that night nearly broke me. But for Juliet, I have prevailed.

I try not to think of it, yet I do remain fearful that perhaps Sergeant Beau Jackson will return, seeking to prove your identity. Yes, it has been four long years, but who knows if we will ever be truly safe? Looking at our precious Juliet, I often think those most fearful thoughts and it drives me to despair. Oh John, I am sorry to share my worries like this, but you must know although I fear for the safety of our child, I fear for yours equally.

You must never return here, ever. Your family has seen to it that you are provided for out there, yet with the knowledge that you must never come back to see them, or me or our child, ever. It is much too dangerous, for all.

Yet, I will continue to tell our Juliet of her handsome father, the one who loves his darling child, the child as you once said to me who "was born for tragedy."

I love you,
Emma

As John finished reading the letter, the agony of the worried words from Emma stung his heart. It was as if a physical blow had lifted him off his feet as he realized he was on his knees. Tears slipped down his face.

"I cannot go on like this any longer." He said to no one, knowing he was utterly alone. "I have been hiding here in Santa Rosa, hiding in the deep forest surrounded with neighbors who swore their loyalty to the confederacy. I have lived here for four years now, supplied with money and shelter by my family, but is this living?"

John got up from his knees, the letter still grasped in his hand. Folding it carefully, he put it inside the wooden box, where he kept all his treasured things. Letters from Asia, a few from his mother and one from Edwin. In four years, that small box was all he had left of his beloved family.

Then he made his way to the kitchen cupboard on the far wall and sought out the comfort in the bottles that lined the shelf. As had become his bad habit, John poured himself one, then two and three drinks of the staunch liquor, waiting for the elixir to take the pain away. It never really took away the loneliness or regret. It only quieted it for a while.

He then went outside to the small front porch that wrapped around the cabin. The only sound was the wind whistling through the tall pines that surrounded his home. But tonight, on a late winter evening, the whisper sound of the wind through the trees was different. He stood motionless and turned his concentration toward what he heard and could not believe his own ears.

It couldn't be!

It was not possible!

A voice. Young and innocent.

The whistling ceased entirely for a moment. In the sudden silence he heard the faint voice of a child calling to him.

"Papa. Please come home."

John could not believe it. He heard it again.

"Papa. It is me, your own Juliet."

John blinked his eyes and shook his head, "This cannot be." But in his heart, he already knew it was real.

Somehow, his beautiful daughter had reached out, sending her need for him and her love through the wind and into his heart.

"Juliet," John cried out into the evening light, "My child," he spread his arms wide, sending up to the sky every bit of his love, "I hear you. Papa is coming home, my sweet Juliet. Your Papa is coming home!"

John stood motionless.

As the wind began it's whistling through the trees again, he knew the magical moment was ending. It had been a gift. Yet his heart yearned for so much more.

He strained to hear the voice again, as he heard ever so faintly in the distant trees, "I love you, Papa."

With that, he knew what he must do. John ran back into the cabin his resolve to see Emma and Juliet pushing him to move at a fevered pitch. "It's time."

He sat down at the well-worn desk and pulled an ancient cane chair to its front as he began to write.

> *Dear sister mine:*
> *"I am coming home…"*

CHAPTER TWENTY

Tudor Hall in Bel Air, Maryland

"Papa, please come home"
~~ Juliet Annabelle Booth

It was early spring, 1870.

While four-year-old Juliet was playing with her cousins Jacob, Joshua and John Joseph, the feeling of sadness suddenly overwhelmed her. For some reason today the comfort of her father's and Aunt Asia's house turned cold. The feeling of loneliness for her father permeated the young girl. She loved to visit the home of her father with Aunt Asia and her cousins who were now aged ten, eight and five.

Sitting on the floor in front of the hearth which crackled and spread warmth to the children laid out in front of it, she suddenly stood and found herself climbing up the stairs to the second floor. The steps under her small feet were swept clean, the wood tones resplendent in the midafternoon sun.

Juliet went in her father's boyhood room, the room directly to the left of the stairs, the one that faced East with the balcony. She stepped to the set of Tudor windows which guarded the entrance and unlatched them. She stepped out on the balcony. The desire and longing to see her father overwhelmed her, as she called his name from out on the balcony with only the wind in the bare trees to hear her plea.

"Papa, please come home, I miss you so. Please come home. Please."

The wind whistled through the early spring trees and nestled near the child as she heard the faint whispering of her father, "My child. I hear you. I am coming home."

But the beautiful sound of her father's voice faded as she heard her frantic mother calling. It stopped the young child and beckoned her to come in off of the balcony.

"Juliet," her mother cried. "Come inside, off of that balcony. You could fall."

Juliet did as her mother asked, returning to the bedroom to face her distraught mother. "Mother," she cried. "I just missed Papa so much. I just had to let him know. I want him home."

Emma bent down to face her beautiful little girl, her skin was white marble like her father's but with the blush tones of her mother. Her eyes black like the longest hour of night, framed by long curled up lashes, also like her father.

Staring into those eyes she remembered the long three days and nights when newborn Juliet did not open her eyes, both parents frantic she could have been blind.

It was John's voice cajoling the baby to open her eyes for the father who loved her so very dearly who she heard. Juliet opened her eyes for the first time. Hers was an exact reflection of his black and mesmerizing gaze, staring back into hers. Emma remembered John's reaction as the tears of relief fell down his cheeks, falling gently upon their beautiful daughter.

Yet she was Emma, too. Her crown of blonde hair fell like pieces of fine silk all about her face and shoulders. The child was a perfect mix of both mother and father.

"Juliet, why did you come up here and out to the balcony?"

The commotion had caused her Aunt Asia and her boys to come to the second floor room. They stood quietly at the entrance, satisfied that Juliet was not injured.

"I just had to call out to Papa, to let him know to please come home." Emma said nothing, just listened. "I heard his voice. He said he was coming home."

Emma's heart lurched at the mention of Juliet's longing, matched only by the pain in her heart, her love and longing for John. Letters deeply lamenting their pain of separation were necessary as to keep him and Emma and Juliet safe, but did little to ease the loneliness of their hearts.

Asia and her oldest son Jacob stepped forward into the room, the mention of hearing John's voice prompting in them a remembrance of a not so long ago cry in the stillness of that early May 1865 night in which both mother and son heard his uncle's agonizing cries that he was alive and to come find him.

Asia went to her niece and said gently, "Child, you said you heard your Papa on the wind?"

"Yes, Auntie Asia, just now. I heard him say he is coming home." Asia looked up at Emma, who was equally dumbfounded. "Papa gave me a gift when I was born to remember him always. He told Mama to say that when I missed him too much, to hold it in my hand and call out to him and he would come."

Asia asked of her niece, "What did your Mother give you?"

Juliet stood firm in her convictions, facing her mother and beloved aunt. She held out her fist and opened it. Around her fingers was laced a gold chain. In it draped a gold medallion.

"The Agnus Dei!" Asia touched it lightly with her fingers. "How did you come by this?"

"Papa gave it me. He took it off his neck and he put it on mine before he went away. I called for him just now. I heard him answer. He is coming home. I know it." Juliet took the gold medallion and put the chain around her neck, dropping it so it was hidden inside her dress.

Jacob came closer, "Juliet," he said gently to his little cousin, "If you say you heard Uncle John, I believe you. Before you were born, I heard him too." He turned to his mother as he said to Asia, "Isn't that right, Mama? Remember?"

Asia looked down at her oldest son and smiled gently, his resemblance to his uncle uncanny as each day passed. "Yes Jacob, I remember she said softly. "I remember."

With that said Jacob took Juliet's hand and led her out of her father's room, down the flight of stairs. The sound of the children's footsteps on the hardwood steps could be heard.

Emma was clearly shaken. "From the time years ago when I darkened the doorway to your home, armed with a letter and the truth, telling you that John was alive and married to me, convincing you to come to Richmond to see him, your belief in me is truly humbling, dear Asia. I have loved you as if we were truly sisters. But you have not told me the reason you have asked us here, now to Tudor Hall."

Asia took a deep breath and said simply, "He's coming home, Emma. Somehow, Juliet knows. He is coming here to Tudor Hall. He wrote to me last winter from his hiding place in the tall forests of California. He was tired of hiding, ready to face the consequences of his terrible deed. That only in this way could he prove his love for you and Juliet by setting you both free."

"He begged me not to tell you, but just to bring you both here and so I have done as he asked. But with Juliet saying she heard his voice? I am so sorry; I didn't know what to do."

Emma pulled away, her hands clenched at her throat at the news. "No," she cried out, "This is not true! Please, I beg you, Asia to tell me he is away and safe. What good will this do now, four years later! What is done cannot be undone. It will solve nothing."

Asia reached into the pocket of her dress and handed Emma a letter. She left it for her sister-in-law to read. As she turned to leave her brother's old room she glanced at the set of Tudor windows that led to the balcony. She could almost hear John's charismatic voice across the years, echoing to her the words of Shakespeare's Romeo and Juliet, a tragic tale.

Emma's hand shook as she held the envelope in her hand. She glanced at it, the writing familiar to her eyes, remembering another letter found in a diary some four years earlier that had been addressed the same then as now, Asia Booth Clarke, Raceway, Philadelphia PA. Her eyes filling with tears she began to read:

Dearest sister Asia:

I am coming home to Tudor Hall. Do not try to talk me out of this as my mind is made up!

As you read this I will already be on my way home. I know you will understand when I tell you this; I have heard my Juliet's voice whispering in the wind that murmurs through the tall pines that serve as my refuge and solace. She wants me to come home. I cannot stay away any longer!

I have been hidden away from my darling wife and sweet baby girl, never seeing them except in my memories in these four long years. Such then tell me, dear sister, is this living? Hiding, hiding always cautious and fearful at every turn, this is no life! For the crime I have committed God will judge me beyond my death. And for the crime I have committed man will judge me here on earth. It is a judgement I cannot and must not elude any longer.

I will go to Washington and tell them all of what happened of who was also behind this conspiracy. And if I am not killed, then I will be by those in the government who know of their involvement and like me, have eluded capture. In this way and only in this way will our family be set free.

Burn your thoughts of me from your memory.

Speak no more of me.

I am coming home, dear sister, to meet my fate and say my farewell. Tell Emma nothing of my plan, it will be like one last sweet surprise that I have come home to Tudor Hall to visit. And you must pretend it is so, for it will be in actuality, the last time I see any of you on earth.

I am not brave and I am not a martyr, but just your brother John who now realizes that is it not enough to be loved, but rather to understand that love sometimes means making sacrifices. So then I will sacrifice my life for the freedom of those I love. I understand this now and so my feet are set on a path that I cannot and will not change.

Think well of me this one last time sister mine, I am coming home to Tudor Hall to see you. Think well of me for the love we shared growing up together. But know that when I am no longer of this earth and your heart is heavy with sadness, go to the balcony in my room, early in the morning as the sun rises, and know as the sunlight touches your face that it is me embracing you with my heart.

Forever yours, Johnny

CHAPTER TWENTY-ONE

Tudor Hall in Bel Air, Maryland

"Let me see your eyes, child of mine"
~~ John Wilkes Booth

Since reading the letter from John to Asia that day, Emma could not sleep. After four long years the idea that John should suddenly decide to turn himself in was more than she could handle. What good would this do now?

She rose from her bed, the humidity of the early spring heat only adding to Emma's anxiety. Her thoughts returned to the Christmas of Juliet's birth when Henry tracked them down in Martinsburg. Emma remembered the name of the home and laughed bitterly, Aurora after the Roman goddess of the dawn.

"Yes," thought Emma, "At first, I thought how fitting the name of the goddess of dawn was, as we were staring a new life together. But like all Roman and Greek Gods, a tragedy would play out."

And so it did. Emma returned to Richmond with baby Juliet and was welcomed back to her childhood home without a scolding or terse word from her mother for leaving in such an abrupt way. Her mother only said upon her return, that a woman's heart is like the ocean, holding vast secrets of love that were not to be shared with anyone. Emma recalled those words now. Perhaps she knew all along the truth of her son-in-law and like Emma would never reveal the secret in her heart.

Not even to her. Nor even to each other.

Henry's was a sad tale, too. His ranting and madness too much for his parents and even old Sam could control. Doctor Hendrix prescribed the mental institution for Henry, one in which he could be watched and taken care of the rest of his life.

After much discussion, Doctor Hendrix agreed to let Old Sam accompany Henry. He had forewarned Old Sam the life at a mental institution was no life for him. He tried to dissuade him, knowing full well the horror of such a place, yet Old Sam refused to relent.

He insisted he must go, saying in his farewell, "See here Doc, I have to stay and take care of him, he is all I got. There ain't no one else I can call my family. I can't ever leave him."

And so, he did stay, standing guard by Henry until the end of their days.

And Beau went back to Durham; she hoped never to be heard from again. She remembered the horror in his eyes as Henry had waved the gun at baby Juliet in the cradle that terrible night. Beau had a wife and child at home. In that moment he thought more of them then the desire to complete Henry's bidding. Yet Emma secretly worried about Beau as he was the one and only one person left who could come back to confront Emma and her secret.

With these dark thoughts in her mind, Emma thought she heard the faint sounds of hooves approaching the isolated farm. Her heart raced as she wondered who it could be. She waited, listened more intently. The sound was unmistakable, it was a single horse. But who could come in the midnight hour to a sleeping house? Only one man. She recalled John's words from long ago when they were fleeing Richmond and her mother's house, "We must leave under the guise of night to Tudor Hall where we will be safe."

Emma covered her mouth with her hands to keep from screaming out her excitement. She ran from her room, flung open the door and heedless of the fact she could barely see past the front lawn, ran towards the sounds of the approaching horse. "John is it you, where are you? Please show yourself. I can barely breathe until I see you!"

In that moment Emma fell to her knees the anticipation shaking her off her feet. With a deliberate stride the figure on the horse seemed to leap off towards Emma, he was dressed in black, his handsome countenance unmistakable, it was her John.

John ran towards Emma and picked her up from her knees. He gathered her up into his arms and kissed her face, her neck, her hands, everywhere he could find.

"Emma, it is you my darling wife. I can't believe I am here touching you seeing you, and soon loving you with all that I am."

"Oh to hear your voice," gasped Emma, "I have missed you so, please tell me this is real and not a dream. I have needed you badly, these past years."

"And I need my wife," John grasped Emma the, lifting her up into his arms and carried her into the house. Her arms laced around his neck as he held her tight. Their time together felt important, every moment precious. He flew up the stairs past his old room and made his way to the bedroom she used that faced over the front lawn.

He closed the door behind them. Emma's breath grew faster with anticipation as she realized John was truly home and he was hers and only hers in that very wanting moment.

She stood next to the bed waiting for her husband. She watched as he took off his hat and started to undress himself in front of her. His eyes were intent on her, black and compelling that were impossible to resist. He divested himself quickly of his clothes and the body revealed was as handsome and irresistible as the first day his eyes captured her.

He stood close to Emma as he slid the nightgown from her body she could feel his breath at her neck as he kissed her lightly, teasing her desire for him. She heard herself whisper to him, "John, please darling, take me. I cannot wait, please darling."

She leaned into her husband as she felt his hand reach for her chin and pull her lips closer to his. He kissed lips gently at first then could not stop himself as his love and desire poured through him, as it was always with her. He thought, "Satisfy my thirst for her, yet leave me thirsty all over again."

He laid her down gently and kissed her lips, her face, and her breasts nestling there then kissing the small of her belly and then further down, pleasuring her until she cried out. He waited as long as he could before he became one with her. Then John loved Emma relentlessly until exhaustion from the long awaited reunion was spent.

Naked and smiling, they lay entwined in the aftermath of their love not wanting to be parted for another moment more.

John rose, sat next to Emma.

His eyes roamed over her body that had become only more lush and beautiful after having had Juliet. His hands could not stay still as he once again stroked her satiny breasts. He savored the feel of them under his hands, her sounds of pleasure arousing his ardor. Without a word between them he kissed her full sweet lips and once again they became as one, their passion for each other like an opiate neither one could resist.

Emma finally chided her husband, "Enough yet?"

John threw his head back and laughed with joy, his black raven curls falling this way and that as he moved. "It could be an eternity dear wife, and even then it would not be enough."

The seriousness of his return tonight weighted heavily on their minds as Emma said, "I wish we could truly be together now until eternity. But Asia told me what you are planning. Nothing can be gained by turning yourself in. What good will it do?"

John stood up beside the bed and began to dress, the aftermath of lovemaking and their heated reunion giving itself over to the deeper meaning of his coming to Tudor Hall.

"Emma, you know I have been hiding in the deep woods in California these four long years with money and supplies from my family keeping me alive. Alive yes, but not living!"

He turned, trying to convince her this was right. "I have to do this. I have the diary and I plan to bring it to Washington myself to prove who I am, to find the men who cajoled me to go through with the assassination and tell the authorities they have the wrong man. I must do this now. Don't you see, I must follow this through, to repent of my crime and to bring all those others who conspired to justice as well."

"I just don't want to lose you again. Please, don't do this."

"In hiding, I had lots of time to think about this. Aisa wrote to me. I know about Henry in the institution after that whole terrible incident at our home in Martinsburg. But what of Beau Jackson, he has disappeared back to North Carolina?"

She nodded. "Perhaps he may once again come after you, we cannot know for sure."

That sealed his determination. "Where there is one slice of doubt of my identity there will be more. This I know and because of this I cannot keep you and Juliet safe. You and Asia sacrificed everything in those early days right after the war because you loved me."

Emma gave into her tears, heartbroken over the situation.

"It is my turn, dear wife, to sacrifice for you, for little Juliet and for my family. It isn't enough to say I love you but to prove it, even if it means sacrificing my life to keep all of you safe. That is what I have learned in my years alone."

Emma was weeping softly as she heard John's explanation, but she still shook her head. "John," she begged, "It will do no good. Please don't do this. Please."

John shook his head, "Where is she my Juliet, my little girl?"

"She is across from your old room."

John crept out of their bedroom then and stood at the door where Juliet slept. He hadn't seen her in four years; the feeling of anticipation overwhelmed him as he opened the door to her room.

The moon shone through the windows, casting a beacon of light upon the child. John stood for a moment and just watched the child breathing softly and evenly like the flutter of angel's wings. He noticed her beautiful blond hair lying about the pillow, so like her mother's. He observed the perfect countenance of her fair face and knew Juliet would be a beauty.

Watching his daughter sleep, he remembered the words of his childhood neighbor Mrs. Rogers years ago when he first brought Emma to Tudor Hall to meet his family. She foretold his child would have the hair and coloring like her mother but would have her father's eyes.

She was right.

He sat on the edge of the bed and whispered as to not frighten the child, "Juliet, it is your father. Open your eyes child and see the father that loves you so."

Her eyes fluttered open. She lay there for a moment. Then she blinked and grinned. "Papa! You came home. I knew you would came home, I just knew it. Oh Papa, I love you so."

Juliet sat up and hugged her father as he kissed her face. He could only say to her, "Let me see your eyes, child of mine, and look at your father who loves you so."

CHAPTER TWENTY-TWO

Tudor Hall in Bel Air, Maryland

"I will return."
~~ John Wilkes Booth

The onset of dawn found John sliding out of the bed he had shared with his wife, staring at his beloved Emma as she slept. He had always held the fear that each time he left her it would be the last.

He sighed deeply with that thought knowing that this time may truly be the last.

Quietly he carefully dressed himself, leaving a folded note on his pillow for his darling. The pillow was still damp as it held the imprint of his face from before he rose and had used the pillow to muffle his deep cries of agony at what may lie ahead.

He closed the door to the bedroom and stepped into the hallway of his boyhood home. Memories flooded his mind's eye as the long ago voices of his youth assailed his heart. He closed his eyes and pictured his room as it was as a young man, the bed with that was covered with the Job quilt that sister Asia had made for him, the bare wood floor under his feet and the room that faced east as to greet the start of another day.

And his balcony, a perfect prop for the ambitious fledging actor and the Shakespearean soliloquies that witnessed his first rehearsals, with only sister Asia and the deep Maryland countryside as an audience.

John opened his eyes then and continued down the stairs past the two-sided hearth in the center of the house and walked out the front door. He breathed in the sweet early morning air imprinting the sights and smells of his last look at home.

After a moment he heard the door behind him open and he turned around.

Standing there was sister Asia and Jacob. The boy had grown, no longer a child. He started to run toward his uncle, but Asia held out a hand to stop him. She stared at her brother and nodded, all the while no smile passing through her lips.

He then turned away as he made his way past the velvety green lawn wet with the morning dew. John heard another voice calling from inside the house.

It was Juliet rushing across the lawn with no shoes upon her feet, her golden hair flying past her shoulders like silken wings.

"Papa, no please. Don't leave!" She cried out as she ran toward her father, "Papa! Please don't go."

John held out his arms to capture his precious Juliet as she rushed to him and leapt up, wrapping herself around him. Crying aloud, small arms clutching his neck, she buried her head into his chest, her tears dripping into his shirt.

He tried to assure his child, "My most precious Juliet, you need to understand that I must take leave of you and you mother and all of the Booth family. I must try to go to Washington to explain the horrible crime I did commit. Darling child, it is for you and my family I do this now."

"But I don't want you to go away again."

"I cannot and will not hide any longer. I must find those who aided me in my crime for they must admit their guilt as well."

John then set her down, leaning down so their faces were at the same height. "Juliet, you cannot fully understand for you are still too young, but someday you will. You see, before you were born, it was your mother and Aunt Asia who sacrificed everything for me in order to protect me so I might live. They did this because they loved me. It is my turn now to sacrifice for all the people I love, your Mother, you, sister Asia and Jacob. All of the Booth family. No one will ever be truly safe until I face the past."

Juliet shook her head and cried, "I don't understand. I am scared that I will never see you again. Please, do not leave us." The child bowed her head as the tears dripped from her dark eyes.

John hesitated for a moment until he noticed something clutched in her hand. "What is it that?"

Juliet opened her hand and tangled in her little fingers was a gold medal on a long chain. It was the Agnus Dei, the Lamb of God, the medal Asia had given John so many years ago. He gasped as he heard his child wise beyond her years, look him into eyes and said in an even and steady voice.

"Papa, you remember this. You gave it to me when I was just a baby. You said if I wanted to see you, to hold onto it and call your name and you would come home."

He was speechless

"You did come, Papa. See, I went to your balcony and called your name. I heard you call mine too."

"Yes, I did come home, my most precious child."

"But I want you to take this now," she offered it, "I want you to wear it." John bowed his head then as his daughter placed the chain around his neck. "If you are in trouble and you need me, hold the medal and call my name and I will find you."

John was kneeling on the damp green carpet of grass facing his sweet little girl. He fingered the medal through his fingers and reached to touch the silken cheek of his precious little girl. He then began to rise from his bent position, as he did he caught the sight of Emma who was pressed up against the large second floor bedroom windows.

He waited there for a moment longer as he watched her unfold a piece of paper and bend her face to read. John drew in a deep breath as he silently read the words he wrote to Emma from his memory.

> *My darlin my darlin my dream my life*
> *Hold fast my love with all your might*
> *Know that although we part and I must leave*
> *You are with me please always believe*
> *That in the darkest of nights and beauty of day*
> *Call my name and I shall pray*
> *And know dearest love I will return*
> *Somehow, someway please do not yearn*
> *For whatever lies ahead you see*
> *Can never erase the you and the me*

Emma then looked up after reading John's words, the tears streaming down her face, her hands pressed up against the glass windows. She was sobbing so violent it wracked her slight body back and forth.

Never moving his gaze from her face, John whispered to his little girl, "Go now child, go to your mother and help ease her heart. Please, hurry now before I change my mine and stay. Hurry, child of mine."

Little Juliet reluctantly turned from her father and ran towards the house to comfort her mother. Emma still stood in the window crying, not wanting to move from it and the lasting sight of her husband.

She then ran her hand across her lower stomach and raised her head higher. All the while John stood transfixed watching her every move.

Emma then murmured to herself, "Perhaps this time dearest God, perhaps this time the child will be a son. For I know today, just as I knew when gifted with our precious Juliet, that I am with child."

She nodded her head to her husband. She stopped crying, her face resolved and determined. She watched as John slowly turned from her and continued over the expansive lawn disappearing into the line of trees that surrounded the pond. She stood at the window until the sounds of her sweet child disrupted the stillness and agony of the room.

It was Juliet who now comforted her mother clinging to her skirts and refraining over and over "It will be alright. Papa will come back, I just know it."

Emma smoothed her child silky hair and murmured to her daughter, and said despondently, "Yes, child I know he will."

Juliet resolved and firm said simply, "Yes he will come back. He will, you see mother, I gave him the medal."

"The medal?" asked Emma.

"Yes," replied Juliet "I gave Papa the Agnus Dei."

The Author, Lisa G. Samia invites you to enjoy reading the historical biographies and her research on the following pages that explain her personal experience writing this fictional story that includes historical photos of John Wilkes Booth, his sister Asia Booth, Clarke, the writer Louisa May Alcott, and the poet Walt Whitman.

Biographies & Author Insights

Louisa May Alcott

The inspiration for "My Name is John Singer" truly came from an unlikely source. I was completely and pleasantly surprised to discover in my research of all things Civil War, that Louisa May Alcott, the author of "Little Women", had worked as a Civil War nurse for about six weeks in Georgetown in Washington DC.

This information availed itself to me in a book penned by Ms. Alcott called "Hospital Sketches." This book or collections of sketches were actually six letters written to Louisa's father while Louisa worked at the Hospital. They are a collection of the author's feelings and observations while working as a duty nurse.

While the sketches detailed her journey to Washington DC and the dismal appearance of our Nation's Capital during the war, there were several descriptions of some of the patients that she nursed that I believe was the center piece of her letters.

There is one sketch however that has stayed with me since the first time I read it and still continues to compel me. It was in my mind the inspiration for "My Name is John Singer."

In this sketch Louisa describes her interaction with a vital and handsome Virginia man named John, with bonny brown hair and eyes like a child.

She quickly realizes her initial observation that his wound was not serious was medically dispelled by the hospital surgeon who regrettably informed her he would die a slow and painful death. It is my understanding that there was an injury to the lung that was fatal.

Louisa was incredulous that such a vital man should die. Resolved to that sobering fact, Louisa sat and nursed John for three days until he passed. Her grief at his passing moved me and touched my heart, as she was holding onto John's hand for such a time after his death, that the Hospital physician came to remind Louisa "It is not good to mingle the living with the dead." She also mentions the imprint of John's grasping hand on hers long after he had passed, vivid and heartbreaking.

So in thinking of the beginnings of "My name is John Singer" Louisa's John and her description of what I could see was a very handsome man and her deep feelings of grief were at the root of this fictional account of John Wilkes Booth. I introduced the fictional Emma Dixon as a nurse working in an Alexandria VA hospital and introduce John Singer as the man hiding in plain sight as John Wilkes Booth.

But because of Louisa's inspiration, I reintroduced her into this story, only her beloved John is now named Jack who is a Virginia blacksmith from nearby Charlottesville, VA. Her interaction with fictional Jack is a love story that was not meant to be, and the agonizing realization of love found and lost.

Louisa's presence in this fictional account has her returning to this hospital at the end of the Civil War to say goodbye to her former co-workers at the hospital and to visit Jack's grave to say farewell once more.

Her presence in the book is one of a kind and deeply compassionate person; it was for me a natural way to write about her based on that one sketch, that one interaction with a certain handsome vital Virginia blacksmith, with the bonny brown hair and eyes of a child.

Their images filled my heart with grief and sorrow yet burned into my thoughts to create such a scene as I brought them both forth to live once again.

Hospital Sketches by Louisa May Alcott (1832-1888). Boston: James Redpath, Publisher, 221 Washington Street, 1863.

Asia Booth Clarke

Asia Booth Clark was the older sister to John Wilkes Booth. History tells us she was about two years old before her parents Junius Brutus Booth, a famous actor and tragedian, and Mary Ann Holmes Booth decided on her name. It was her father Junius who initially thought Aisha after the Prophet Muhammed's favorite and youngest wife and her middle name as Frigga because she was born on a Friday. They eventually agreed on Asia Frigga Booth.

She was simply put; a sensitive young woman given to "sulks" yet by all accounts was a loving and devoted sibling and daughter. Her insights found in her book "The Unlocked Book, A Memoir of John Wilkes Booth" were laced with her memories and recollection of her life on the family farm at Tudor Hall in Bel Air, Maryland. Her description of her brother John, just two year younger were also invaluable insights into the young John Wilkes Booth. They were extraordinarily close and remained so even after they left the farm at Tudor Hall.

It was these vivid descriptions of her brother John on the farm when they were young that revealed to me a John Wilkes Booth I have never known.

History tells us of the heinous deed he committed when assassinated President Lincoln, yet that was all I knew of him. It was Asia and her writings that showed a unexplored side of John, the disconnect for me between him growing up as a loving son, sibling, friend and great actor to committing what could possibly be the most heinous act in American History, was one in which for me had no explanation. It still does not.

Because of Asia' love of her brother John, in my fictional account, I have brought Asia into the story with her not wanting to believe her loving brother John could have committed such an act; even though all facts state he was murdered at Garrett's Farm.

The suffering I have brought forth in Asia is what I believe is the pain she actually went through after his horrendous deed. However, in my fictional account, I brought both brother and sister to meet once again with "John Singer" prevailing upon his sister Asia that he was indeed alive and tried to explain to her the unexplainable.

In this adaptation, I have Asia as forgiving to her brother and his crime, working to find a way to help hide him and continue to keep him alive. Her great ability to forgive his deed, expose herself and family to treason, was in fact for me an adventure into that part of her. I believed she loved John above and beyond his crime.

But History tells us her grief was inconsolable. Asia left the United States in 1868 with her husband John Sleeper Clarke and her children, Asia, Edwin, Adrienne, Clarke, Lillian, Wilfred and Joan to reside in the English countryside.

Her children in my account are purely fictional.

Unfortunately her life there was not a happy one, isolated from her family in the United States and a growing isolation with her husband. She died at the age of fifty two in 1888.

Her last request to her children was to be buried in the United States at Greenmount cemetery in Baltimore Maryland, where the Booth family had their plot. Specific to her last request of being buried there, she was laid to rest next to her brother John who is buried there in the Booth plot in an unmarked grave.

Asia Frigga Clarke née Booth (November 19, 1835, Bel Air, Maryland – May 16, 1888, Bournemouth, England)

Clarke, Asia Booth. THE UNLOCKED BOOK: A MEMOIR OF JOHN WILKES BOOTH BY HIS SISTER.... New York: 1938. 1st ed., 205p., ft., plates. [M3611] Asia Booth Clarke's memoir of her brother John Wilkes Booth has been recognized as the single most important document available for understanding the personality of the assassin of Lincoln.

Walt Whitman

Walt Whitman's presence in John Singer as himself, writer and sometimes nurse during the Civil War, was for me a journey brought forth from his interaction with President Lincoln.

Although history tells us he never met President Lincoln, he saw him some twenty or thirty times during his Presidency riding through Washington DC or to his summer retreat at the Soldier's Home.

His description of their meetings was summed up by Whitman stating "I see the President almost every day," he wrote in the summer of 1863. "We have got so that we exchange bows, and very cordial ones." Once Lincoln gave Whitman a long friendly stare. "He has a face like a Hoosier Michael Angelo," Whitman wrote, "so awful ugly it becomes beautiful, with its strange mouth, its deep cut, criss-cross lines, and its doughnut complexion."

There was, Whitman wrote, "a deep latent sadness in the expression." He was "very easy, flexible, tolerant, almost slouch, respecting the minor matters," but capable of "indomitable firmness (even obstinacy) on rare occasions, involving great points."

He was a family man but had an air of complete independence: "He went his own lonely road," Whitman said, "disregarding all the usual ways—refusing the guides, accepting no warnings—just keeping his appointment with himself every time." His "composure was marvelous" in the face of unpopularity and great difficulties during the war.

He had what Whitman saw as a profoundly religious quality. His "mystical foundations" were "mystical, abstract, moral and spiritual," and his "religious nature" was "of the amplest, deepest-rooted, loftiest kind." Summing Lincoln up, Whitman called him "the greatest, best, most characteristic, artistic, moral personality" in American life.

It was this admiration for the President and especially the line "a deep latent sadness in the expression", that was remarkable in its vivid imagery of Lincoln. So much so, that I brought forth Walt Whitman in my fictional account as to continue the saga of Mr. Whitman's' pain at the assassination of the President and to show his inconsolable grief.

In my fictional account, it was Mr. Whitman that initially believed that John Singer could be John Wilkes Booth.

Through his grief and defense of the President, Mr. Whitman called out to John Singer his incredible resemblance to John Wilkes Booth. His moving poem recited to "John Singer," "Oh Captain! My Captain!" about the death of Lincoln was important. I again brought forth as to strengthen his resolve to the loss of President Lincoln as well as his grief over the loss of so many in the Civil War.

Walt Whitman and his words and actions inspired me as I moved forward to create this story. His ability with his writing to make me see the pain he so eloquent describes in the President's eyes was for me too moving and heartbreaking not to once again try to bring back to life.

Walt Whitman- Occupation Journalist, Poet (May 31, 1819 - March 26, 1892)
David S. Reynolds, The Gilder Lehrman Institute of American History –Lincoln and Whitman

John Wilkes Booth

While History tells us that John Wilkes Booth acted alone (albeit in conjunction with several conspirators) to decapitate the Government at the end of the Civil War, in my fictional account I have placed the secret Confederate Society the Knights of the Golden Circle at the helm of this most horrifying deed. Also, in this fictional account Booth is repentant for the crime he committed, something of course History tells us not true.

Yet in all the research and reading I did preparing to write this story, a nagging feeling prevailed upon me, in such a way that the disconnect from John's youth to becoming a young actor was growing wider and wider as I read of how incensed he was of President Lincoln, the defeat of the south and the freeing of the slaves.

Yes, he was a southern sympathizer most assuredly, yet the path traveled from a loving sibling, son, friend and highly regarded actor to moving forward to plan, conspire and follow through to assassinate the President was most assuredly a path of life choices that once again to me left me with more questions than answers.

History tells us John was the favorite of the Booth household, the ninth of ten children born to Junius and Mary Ann Booth. He was a lover of animals, poetry and nature. As an adult, John watched in horror as a man in a wagon beat his horse while trying to move him from the mud. John saw this and punched the man for beating the animal.

Also one day, upon leaving Ford's Theater in costume on his way to the telegraph office, saw a small boy lost perhaps but plainly poor, John picked up the small child to him, hugged him, stood him up and gave him a few coins before running on his way.

Another story of his compassion for others is told in which an equally poor young boy selling programs at Ford's Theater was shivering in the cold. John came upon the boy and took him to the haberdasher's to fit in a proper news cap to keep the child warm.

And it is recorded that with sister's Asia' children, having placed a picture of himself above their beds and John reminded them to "Pray for me babies."

These and instances like these prevailed through my thoughts as I prepared to write his story.

There are still theories that believe he did escape the barn that another confederate sympathizer took his place, and there was a government cover-up to that effect. All theories without historical proof.

Again, these are questions without any real answers.

In order for my story to work, I in turn called upon various theories, writing that John escaped the barn at Garrett's farm, and was hiding in plain sight in an Alexandria, VA hospital. Or was he?

In this fiction, Booth is repentant for his crime, suffering silently in recounting the actions that led him to the hospital, asking God if it was by some trick of fate he was alive.

He does of course realize his fate to hide in plain sight. The uniform he stole from the dead confederate on his flight out to the barn will forever now cause him to be known as John Singer. His family is dead to him, all those who knew and loved him he would never see again. Lost forever for the crime he so boldly committed.

He was for me and remains one of the most compelling and complicated men in American History. In this fictional account, both his sister Asia and the fictional Emma Dixon risk their lives to save him and protect him. And in this sequel we see John willing to risk his life to save them.

It is at best, quite the "what if"!

John Wilkes Booth (May 10, 1838-April 26,1865)

Lisa G. Samia

<u>www.LisaSamia.com</u>
FB: Lisa G. Samia
Instagram: authorlisasamia
Twitter: @LisaSamia

Author, Award Winning Poet and Speaker

The Nameless and the Faceless of the Civil War a collection of 28 poems and 28 essays named FINALIST in 2018 & 2019 National Parks Arts Foundation Artist in Residence –Gettysburg Poetry

The Man with the Ice Blue Eyes –a collection of love poems debuted number one Amazon.com for poetry for women July 2016.

Two poems in the collection earned 2 poetry awards from the CT Authors and Publishers Association

Lectured at Blenheim, Civil War Interpretive Center-Fairfax VA CT Civil War Round Table

The Doctor Samuel A. Mudd House Museum-Waldorf MD

The Edgar Allen Poe House museum in Baltimore MD and the Poe Museum in Richmond VA

Originally from Boston MA, Lisa now resides in Avon CT with her husband Jim. Attended the University of Massachusetts in Boston

Member of the following Historical Societies:

Ford's Theater, Washington, DC
Lincoln Cottage, Washington, DC
The Surratt Society, Clinton, MD
The Junius Brutus Booth Society (Tudor Hall), Bel Air, MD
The Civil War Trust
The Doctor Samuel A. Mudd Society, Waldorf MD
The Avon Historical Society, Avon, CT
Civil War Round Table, CT
The Poe Museum-Richmond VA
The Poe House-Museum Baltimore MD
The American Civil War Museum, Richmond VA

HISTORICAL PHOTO CREDITS

John Wilkes Booth –
Wikipedia /
https://en.wikipedia.org/wiki/John_Wilkes_Booth
Wikimedia Commons
https://commons.wikimedia.org/wiki/Category:John_Wilkes_B
ooth
https://commons.wikimedia.org/wiki/Category:John_Wilkes_B
ooth#/media/File:John_Wilkes_Booth_1865.jpg
https://commons.wikimedia.org/wiki/Category:John_Wilkes_B
ooth#/media/File:John_Wilkes_Booth_cph.3a26098.jpg
https://commons.wikimedia.org/wiki/Category:John_Wilkes
_Booth#/media/File:John_Wilkes_Booth_CDV_by_Black_%26
_Case.jpg
HistoryNet.com http://www.historynet.com/john-wilkes-
booth

Asia Booth Clarke – Wikipedia / Wikimedia Commons
BoothieBarn https://boothiebarn.com/picture-
galleries/booth-family/asia/

Walt Whitman –Wikipedia / Wikimedia Commons
https://commons.wikimedia.org/wiki/File:Whitman_at_abou
t_fifty.jpg
https://commons.wikimedia.org/wiki/Walt_Whitman

Louisa May Alcott –Wikipedia / Wikimedia Commons
https://commons.wikimedia.org/wiki/Louisa_May_Alcott#/
media/File:Louisa_May_Alcott_headshot.jpg
Province Public Library --
http://www.provlib.org/news/coming-falllouisa-may-alcott-
woman-behind-little-women

*Historical Letter to Mary Ann Holmes Booth pg 17
Source -- "Right or Wrong, God Judge Me" The Writings of
John Wilkes Booth Edited by John Rhodehamel and Louis Taper
1977 by The Board of Trustees of the University of Illinois (page
144-145)

**Page 17
Source -- "Right or Wrong, God Judge Me" The Writings of
John Wilkes Booth Edited by John Rhodehamel and Louis Taper
1977 by The Board of Trustees of the University of Illinois (page
144-145)

9 781943 504343